Chapter One

The Beachcomber

A bitter dawn broke over the streets of the brown city. Red streaks appeared in the grimy sky. Rats, hump-backed and squeaking, slid like shadows from heaps of rubbish and disappeared into the drains. The last gusts of a November storm flung leaves across the squares and blew the river into waves. In the great jostling harbour, steamers and sailing ships tugged at their moorings.

A warren of warehouses and shabby streets rose steeply above the docks. At one corner, above a high and sooty brick wall, a faded notice proclaimed:

S. Fisher
Rags and Bones

A bolt rattled sharply and tall black gates swung open.

A skinny boy emerged, pushing a handcart. For a moment he stood, beaten by the wind, looking down on the forest of nodding masts and rigging. Then he grasped the handles of his cart, hunched his shoulders and started along the still-dark street.

His name was Silas. He was a quick, sharp-featured boy, a street urchin. Newly-risen from bed, he was dirty. Uncombed hair hung about his face. Those of his clothes that were not too large were too small, and all were ragged. Padding burst from the shoulder of a man's jacket, bare feet showed through cracks in a pair of heavy boots. People called him Young Silas, to distinguish him from Old Silas, his grandfather, with whom he lived.

He was heading for the seashore almost a mile away. The cart wheels rattled along sleeping cobbles. Poor houses and shops – breadshops, pawnshops, taverns – rose on either hand. The streets were deserted. Only an old lamplighter with a pole moved from gas-lamp to gas-lamp, trailing the grey half-light of dawn in his wake.

As Silas emerged from the shelter of houses into the teeth of the gale, his eyes watered, his jacket flapped wildly. Below him lay the larger of two great breakwaters that curved like pincers about the harbour mouth. The lighthouse flashed one – two – three times. The foaming sea, more white than dark, flung itself against the walls and exploded in plumes of spray.

Battling against the wind, Silas broke into a run that took him on to a high promenade above the shore. Cliffs fell sheer beneath him. He paused to take in the scene then hurried along and soon a steep street, lined with fishermen's cottages and smelling of fish and tar, descended in twisting bends to the lower promenade. Silas parked his cart by a boat-builder's yard, squeezed through the promenade rails, and dropped three metres to the sand.

The tide was on the ebb. A tangled ribbon of weed and flotsam lay along the beach. Later in the morning the shore would be alive with beachcombers, poor folk squabbling over fish boxes and lengths of net cast up by the storm. But Silas came first. He unwound a sack from his waist and felt the bite of the wind.

It was a rewarding dawn. Almost at once he discovered the head of a broom with most of the bristles remaining. He gathered scraps of wood that could be dried and chopped and sold as kindling. He found a shoe and a seaman's boot, an ornamental bottle, a plank, and a length of rope that was almost new. Carefully he stripped off the clinging weed and dropped them into his sack.

He shivered, turning his thin back to the wind, and fastened a tear in his trousers with a scrap of wire.

Slowly daylight was strengthening. Silas gazed along the shore. A short distance ahead something white or silver glinted among the tumbled weed. Hoisting the sack and plank to his shoulder, he headed towards it.

As he came nearer he saw that it was the tail of a great fish, scarred red by a beating on the rocks. Quickly he ran forward and tumbled his burden to the sand.

What kind of fish it was Silas could not say, for its front half was hidden among weed. Whatever it was, however, if it was still fresh it would provide several fine meals for his grandfather and himself. He could sell cutlets in the street later that morning. Eagerly he tugged the seaweed aside.

What happened next gave Silas the biggest fright of his young life. The great tail flapped weakly. Without any warning a white arm shot out of the weed and struck at his face. Long nails that would have sliced him to the bone flashed past his cheek. With a cry he jumped back.

The sudden movement had disturbed the weed. Gazing down, Silas saw a girl's face: wild eyes and white teeth. His heart thudded. Open-mouthed, he gazed from her face to the elegant tail and back again.

"Ssssss!" she hissed warningly.

Not wishing to come into contact with those nails, Silas seized his plank and began to rake the weed aside. The girl tried to cover herself but she was no match for the quick boy. In a minute her side lay bare from shoulder to tail.

The bitter wind and roar of the sea persuaded Silas that he was not dreaming. He had heard sailors tell stories of mermaids but never really believed in them. Now here one lay before him, washed up by the November storm. From head to waist she had the body of a girl, and below the waist the tail of a fish. She was young and she was savage and she was beautiful. Clearly, also, she was badly hurt, for her shoulder was bruised purple and a cut on her forehead oozed blood into her long hair that lay matted among the weed and sand.

With a glittering gaze she regarded him.

Silas did not know what to do. He crouched and reached nervously to touch her silver tail. "I'm not going to hurt you," he said, as one would speak to a frightened but alarming dog.

"Ssssss!" The tail lashed out, a blow that would have broken his arm. "Beware!" she hissed. "I am danger-ous!"

But as her tail fell to the sand the mermaid could not repress a cry of pain.

"You're injured!" Silas exclaimed. "I don't want to harm you, I want to help."

The mermaid stared into his face, then up and down the deserted beach.

"Are you alone?"

"Yes."

The sea crashed and surged towards them.

The mermaid sank back upon the weed. Her eyes closed for a moment.

"Can I trust you?"

"Yes," Silas said.

Her gaze wandered over his ragged clothes. "You are not a rich boy. You could sell me for much money, put me in a cage, show me in fairgrounds."

"Sell you! Put you in a cage!" Silas wrinkled his brow. "How could I do that? You're a – a mermaid!"

A fleeting smile crossed her face. "If you truly wish to help," she said, "then hide me until I am recovered and can return to the sea. The waves are rough and my strength has gone."

"Hide you!" Silas gazed from the promenade to the wave-swept rocks along the beach. "Where? In two hours the shore will be full of fishermen and beach-combers. The children explore every cave." He thought. "The only place I know is the scrapyard at home. We could go there if you like. You'd be safe with me and Granda."

"The scrapyard," she repeated. "It sounds very different from my home. Is it far from the sea?"

"It's close to the harbour."

"And how would I get there?"

"I could take you on the cart." Silas pointed along the beach. "If I cover you with weed I can be back in ten minutes."

"Our journey – does it lie through the streets?"

He nodded.

The mermaid's eyes closed. "Very well – otherwise I shall die. But it must be a secret. Tell no one, not even a friend." She clutched his wrist. "Promise!"

"No, never!" His eyes were wide.

They scooped a hollow in the sand and pebbles and the mermaid lay in it. She did not appear to feel the cold but Silas's fingers ached as he heaped the wet weed on top until her sandy skin and silver tail were hidden.

"Remember," came a muffled voice. "My life is in your hands."

"I have promised!" Silas said.

Quickly he covered his plank and beachcombing sack and ran back along the seashore. The jacket flapped about his skinny chest. Sand had leaked into his iron-hard boots and chafed his feet.

Growing daylight revealed the waste of seas. Low clouds scudded overhead. Far along the beach tiny figures had appeared, hunting along the tide-line. A stooped winkle-gatherer carried her bucket among the bitter rock pools. On the cliff-top promenade early workmen lowered their heads into the wind.

Silas mounted a steep ramp from the beach. His knuckles were blue, his face pinched with the cold. Quickly he seized the handles of his cart and started back the way he had come.

Soon he stood once more above the heaped seaweed. It was hard to believe that a *mermaid* lay hidden there.

"It's only me." He looked up and down the beach. "All's clear. Don't be frightened."

The weed stirred and the mermaid's face peered up through the strands.

"Quick," Silas said. "Get up on the cart. You'll have to help, I can't lift you by myself."

It was a painful struggle, but the mermaid was brave and soon lay on the splintered boards.

"It smells!" She wrinkled her nose distastefully.

Silas flushed. "I'd better tie you on." He reached into his sack for the new-found length of rope. "It'll be a bumpy ride."

The mermaid regarded him apprehensively and curled her tail up over the edge of the cart. Silas threw coils of rope across and tugged them tight. Then he piled weed on top and weighted it down with his beach-combing sack and morning finds.

"Are you all right?"

"I think so."

"Right, here we go." He took the handles. "Hold tight."

The ebbing tide had packed the sand hard but still the wheels sank. Boots skidding, Silas pushed and tugged his cart around an outcrop of rocks and up the beach. A wooden ramp led to a huddle of boat sheds on the lower promenade. Silas gritted his teeth and heaved, but no matter how he struggled, he could not haul his weighted cart from the shore.

"Hang on, shipmate, I'll give you a hand."

A cheery young sailor swung a sea-chest from his shoulder and strode down the ramp. Strong hands grasped the handles and soon the cart was safely on the promenade.

"Thanks, Jack Tar." Silas gave an urchin grin.

"You're welcome, lad." The sailor clapped the boy's back and strode on.

Silas pushed his cart along the promenade and started up the twisting road that led to the cliff top. Early smoke rose from the chimneys of the fishermen's cottages on either hand. Many were poor, a few boasted white railings and bull's-eye windows. The climb was a struggle but at length the road levelled out high above the sea.

Soon Silas was back in the wilderness of narrow streets that ran above the docks.

The city was coming to life. Sleepy pie-boys carried trays covered with white cloths. Yawning carters led horses on bridles. The scent of fresh bread blew from alleyways. Curtains were drawn back; shop doors were opening; shrill voices were raised in a quarrel.

Silas took little notice. The wheels of his handcart rattled along the cobbles.

" 'Ere! What's that?" A fat woman in an apron was

pointing. "What's that 'anging over the edge o' your cart?"

Silas spotted it as she spoke. A long silver tail trailed halfway to the ground. Clumsily he heaved it from sight.

"What is it?" the woman insisted.

Silas was used to the quick ways of the streets. "Mermaid," he said cheekily. "What d'you think!"

"A mermaid!" The woman shook her fist. "You cheeky young ha'porth. I'll mermaid you! A big skate, more like, or a nice fresh 'alibut. Come round this way after you've cut it up and I'll buy two fillets."

"Righto, Ma. See you later." Silas hurried on.

Soon the crowded harbour lay beneath him. A sheet of newspaper whirled past on the wind. To and fro, to and fro, his grandfather's sign swung on the corner.

A little black cat, scarcely more than a kitten, watched from the gateway of the rag-and-bone yard as he drew close.

"Come on, Sweep." Silas made a kissing noise. "Good puss."

The little cat pressed about his ankles, then suddenly danced round in mad circles of play and shot back through the entrance. Silas followed it into the yard, clashed the big gates shut and dropped the locking bar in place.

The yard was filled with junk.

Half hidden by shadows, a kindly face peered from the

window of the house. It was his grandfather. Old Silas was sick and had been for some time. The November fogs got into his bones. Throughout the night he had sat up coughing. His forehead was damp with perspiration, his cheek white with stubble.

"Granda!" Silas shouted. "Granda! Come and see what I found on the beach."

Quickly he pushed his treasures aside and tumbled armfuls of weed to the ground.

Beneath the criss-crossed ropes the mermaid lay still. Her wild eyes were closed, matted hair trailed over one shoulder. She was quite unconscious.

Chapter Two

Jasper Dredge

Silas and his grandfather carried the mermaid indoors. Old Silas cleaned her wounds with salt water for they had started to bleed again. Then they laid her on a ragged settee and covered her with a blanket.

The old man was astonished. "Tell me again how you found her," he said.

Silas had not eaten that morning. He cut a wedge of bread and poured a cup of water from the black kettle that steamed on the fire.

"Will it be long before she wakes up, Granda?" he said when he had finished his story.

"No way of knowing." Old Silas held thin hands towards the flames. "Ten minutes, ten hours. She looks weary, poor thing."

Silas tore at his crust with white teeth.

The living-room, the only downstairs room in the

house, was large. It was bare and brown, with a single window and two doors, one leading to the yard, the other to an empty hall and staircase to the bedrooms above. Crooked beams, hung with old harness and lengths of net, oilskins, broken chairs and other assorted objects, crossed the ceiling. Splintered floorboards were partly covered by a threadbare rug. All their cooking was done on the fire. Each morning Silas filled a bucket with bright water from a pump in the street.

Only one item of furniture, a grandfather clock, was not shabby and rickety. It had been made by an ancestor and was Old Silas's pride and joy.

Sweep sprang down from Silas's lap. The little cat was fascinated by the mermaid. Lightly it leaped to the foot of the settee. An end of silver tail protruded from the blanket. Delicately the cat sniffed and tugged with needle-sharp claws.

"Hey, Sweep!" Silas jumped up laughing. "That's not a fish. Stop it!"

But before he could catch his pet the mermaid stirred in her sleep. The long tail twitched and Sweep was sent flying across the room. Startled, the little cat stood blinking with round yellow eyes.

With a whirr and mellow chime the grandfather clock struck nine.

"I'll take that load across the harbour this morning," Silas said.

"Don't let that warehouseman cheat you again," said his grandfather. He glanced at the settee. "Don't worry about the lass here. I'll keep an eye on her."

Silas massaged his bare toes at the hearth and thrust them back into his cracked boots. "I might as well go now." He drank off the last of the hot water and set his cup on the high mantelpiece.

The day had brightened. It took all Silas's strength to load six bundles of rags the size of himself on to the handcart, and stop it from running away as he descended the steep street.

The harbour smelled of salt and tar, rope and wood, and a hundred foreign ports. Mountains of cargo stood on the quays: rum from the Americas, spices from the Indies, casks and crates and bales stacked high as houses. Silas made his way between them and along the thronging wharfs. Ships rocked at their moorings, rigging shook and smoke streamed in the wind.

"Hello there, Silas." A sailor greeted him. "Bit breezy, eh!"

Silas loved the busy harbour, but his thoughts remained with the mermaid as he pushed his cart past bowling casks and swinging nets of cargo. Soon he reached a sheltered backwater where ferrymen moored the little craft that plied busily across the open water.

He loosened a painter from an iron ring and pulled his grandfather's boat to the quayside. It was an open boat called the *Sea Urchin*, much used and badly in need of a coat of paint. Oars and mast and a patched sail were lashed neatly along one side.

Silas lowered his bundles of rags on a rope, then descended a flight of weedy steps set into the quay. He cast off and soon was bobbing beneath hanging anchors and the hulls of ships that towered overhead. Easily he pulled on the oars and headed out into the middle of the harbour. The breakwaters checked the force of the sea, but the wind was strong and blew the water into choppy waves. Spray whipped up from the blades of his oars and Silas had to pull harder to avoid being blown up-river. Then the current tried to take him downstream and out to sea. But Silas was used to the tricks of the tide. Red-cheeked, the hair blown from his brow, he approached a muddy slipway on the opposite shore.

The cargo was soon off-loaded and lugged on a heavy barrow to the rag warehouse, a short distance from the water's edge in a maze of dirty streets.

"Stack them up there."

A mean-faced man with narrow eyes pointed to a multi-coloured pile in a far corner.

"That's your job." Silas disliked the warehouseman. "I just deliver them."

"Cheeky young devil!" The man struck a blow at the boy's head.

Silas dodged and held out a hand for payment.

Reluctantly the man pulled out a greasy bag and dropped some coins into his palm. Carefully Silas counted them.

"That's twopence short!"

"Twopence short, is it? Well, you must have dropped it or had a pint of ale on your way home, mustn't you." The warehouseman laughed.

"You wait till my Granda hears about this!" Silas cried.

"Your Granda! Old Silas Fisher! He's sick, everyone knows that. Die most likely!" The man turned away. "Good riddance, an' all."

Sickened, Silas made his way from the warehouse.

A fat man with a check waistcoat and bushy red beard stood in the entrance. Idly he leaned against the doorpost and cleaned his nails with a pocket knife. His name was Jasper Dredge. He was a dangerous man, well-known in the city. A yellow mongrel, a savage-looking creature with a huge head, stood at his heels.

Flushed with anger at the warehouseman's words, Silas took little notice. But as he walked past, Jasper thrust out a foot. Silas tumbled full length, his money scattered. Before he could rise the fat man set a foot in the middle of his back.

"You stay there," he snarled, "else it'll be the worse for you!"

With quick fingers he gathered up the coins and

dropped them into a waistcoat pocket.

"There, right. You can get up now." He snorted. "Stand me a couple o' drinks, that will. Now be off – afore I set the dog on you."

At this the starved mongrel growled and showed its teeth.

Silas picked himself up and brushed the mud from his jacket. Slowly he walked away. But when he had gone a short distance he halted and picked a fist-sized rock from the gutter. The fat man had turned his back and was talking to the warehouseman.

"Hey!" Silas called boldly. "Jasper Dredge!"

Jasper turned to face him.

"You fat pig!" Silas cried. "Thief! Coward!"

He drew back his arm and flung the rock. It was a splendid shot and bounced off the man's head. Luckily he was wearing a battered top hat, which went flying, for otherwise the rock would have knocked him senseless.

Jasper uttered a great roar.

"Why, you –!"

He began to run but was no match for the speedy boy.

"Go on, Bosun!" He urged his dog forward. "Sic 'im! Sic 'im!"

The dog ran half a dozen metres and planted its feet, barking ferociously. It was an ugly animal, outrageously ugly, with wiry yellow hair and the wrinkled face of a bulldog.

From a corner a safe distance away, Silas looked back.

"Go on, you brute!" Jasper yelled. "Sic 'im! Tear 'is throat out!"

But the alarming dog did not pursue the boy. In fury Jasper struck it across the head with his fist and drew back his boot. The dog yelped and cowered to the ground.

"Useless 'ound!" the fat man raged. "For two pins I'd send you to the glue factory!"

Silas waited to see no more. Muttering at the loss of his money, he returned to the boat by a roundabout route.

Rubbish lay against the walls of the warehouses. As Silas approached the slipway, a huge rat, big as a cat, scuttled from a pile of decaying timbers. He flung a piece of brick and chased it to the water's edge. With a plop the rat dived into the harbour. Silas craned forward to see it, sleek and long-tailed, swimming into one of the open drains that carried the water from the city. He threw several more stones, splashing on all sides, but none hit and soon the rat was gone from sight.

Silas collected the boat and rowed back across the harbour.

Scraps of driftwood bobbed among straw and other flotsam in sheltered corners of the quays. He collected them as he returned to his mooring, and lugged them up the treacherous steps. Like the wood he had gathered on the shore, they could be dried and chopped and sold in bundles as kindling.

But as Silas pushed his cart up the steep street, his thoughts were far from firewood. He scowled at the memory of Jasper Dredge and the dishonest warehouseman – it had taken days and weeks to collect those bundles of rags. Then he thought of the mermaid and his face brightened. Had she woken yet?

She had not. Her wild eyes were still closed in sleep. Her long hair had dried on the rough blanket. She was dreaming, for her brow was furrowed and every so often she emitted a little cry or broken words.

"Poor lass, she's had a hard time," said his grandfather.

"Will she be all right?"

"A good sleep's the best thing in the world for her."

The old man handed Silas a plate of eel and potatoes from the side of the fire. As he ate it he told his grandfather how he had been cheated and robbed.

"Jasper Dredge!" Old Silas was angry. "If only I had my strength again."

"Don't worry, Granda." Silas grinned cheerfully and showed the muscles in his skinny arm. "I'm getting bigger all the time. In a few years no one will be able to cheat us."

"Indeed they won't." The old man rumpled his grandson's hair.

"I'll make a lot of money so you can afford the best doctors in the world. Then we'll go somewhere warm where your chest will get better. And when we come back we'll buy a horse."

"So we will." Old Silas coughed convulsively. "You're a fine lad. I'm proud of you."

"And you're the best granda in the world."

"I'm afraid I'm not, Silas, but I'd like to be." He stretched cold hands towards the fire. "I'm not looking forward to this winter."

As if in response to his words the wind whined about the house. On the settee the mermaid gave a stifled cry and tossed her head from side to side. A bitter draught blew around their ankles and made the fire leap.

Chapter Three

Rags and Bones

"**R**ags and bones!" Shrill as a seagull, Silas pushed his cart towards the city centre. "Any ra-a-gs and bo-o-nes!"

It was early afternoon. His cries mingled with the shouts of vendors in the busy streets. The iron-clad wheels rattled on cobbles. Puddles and straw hid lurching potholes.

Silas had a regular round. This day it took him through the thronging heart of the city to the houses of the gentry which lay beyond.

Here life was different: flower beds, neatly planted for spring, lay beneath the naked trees; polished lamps winked beside painted doors; scrubbed steps descended to broad pavements.

"Rags and bones! Bring out your rags and bo-o-o-nes!"

Every so often a back door or kitchen window opened and he was summoned. "Hey! Boy!" Having been bossed about all day, the servants spoke imperiously. "Wait here!" Silas waited and several minutes later they emerged with a mangle broken beyond repair, or a huge ham bone from which every last ounce of nourishment had been boiled. "There!" Contemptuously, as if conferring a favour, they handed it down and dusted their fingers as if to remove the grime which came from proximity to the ragboy.

"Thank you kindly." Silas set the article in his cart and moved on up the square. "Rags and bones! Any ra-a-gs and bo-o-o-nes!"

Throughout the afternoon, as his cracked voice rang against the façades of the grand houses, Silas's thoughts remained with the mermaid. Had she woken yet? What was she eating? What were she and his grandfather talking about?

"Pssst!" A kitchen girl, poor as Silas himself and little older, summoned him from a flight of steps below street level. "Here." Guiltily, with backward glance lest she was seen by the cook, she thrust a stale roll and slice of cold bacon into his hands and ran back to her work. With a quick smile she looked up from the door.

"Thank you," Silas said.

A loud voice called from the kitchen beyond. The door shut hastily, the girl was gone.

Silas continued along the street. "Rags and bo-o-nes!" Crumbs blew from his lips.

Carriages rattled past. Flower sellers stood at their pitches; errand boys delivered poultry and groceries; a stooped old woman with a shovel and sack scraped horse dung from the cobblestones. A lady on the arm of a gentleman touched a perfumed handkerchief to her nose as they walked by.

The air grew colder. Far away, beyond the elegant squares and belching factory chimneys that lined the horizon, the sky turned orange with dusk. Silas blew on his knuckles.

"Rags and bones! Bring out your ra-a-gs and bo-o-o-nes!"

A lamplighter moved along the street with his rod. Behind him a line of gaslights glittered against the gathering darkness.

Pushing his handcart more briskly, Silas hurried through the rest of his round. By the time he had finished it was evening. The streets had emptied. In the houses of the rich the curtains were drawn; fires blazed and lamps shone in comfortable drawing-rooms. His toes frozen, Silas turned for home. It had not been a bad day's collecting. Despite the late start his cart was half full.

In the city centre theatres glowed invitingly. Flower sellers and chestnut roasters sat late; the savour of pies rose from trays above glowing charcoal. Silas had no money for such luxuries.

The fine buildings were left behind. As he drew near the harbour the streets grew poorer.

"Well! Silas Fisher! Rag-and-bone man!"

It was Albert Dredge, Jasper's son, an old enemy. He was a fat youth, several years older than Silas. His cheeks were full, his eyes were small. Thick lips opened to reveal yellow, inward-sloping teeth. He wore a battered deerstalker and a red neckerchief. Like his father he was a brute and a bully. Fortunately he had not yet heard of the incident on the far side of the river.

"What've we got 'ere, then?"

With thieving, impertinent hands he turned over the goods in Silas's cart.

"You leave them alone!" Silas set the cart on its legs and ran to stop him.

"Watch yourself, sonny!" Albert pushed him back with a thick hand. "What's this, then?" Tumbling aside a cushion and pair of broken pram wheels, he pulled out a gentleman's shirt. It was the best find of the day.

"Give it back!" Silas made a grab. Albert twitched the shirt from his reach and held it out.

"Yer. That'll do me very nicely." He began to stuff it inside his jacket.

With a cry Silas flung himself upon the older boy, kicking and punching. For a time they scuffled, but he was no match for Albert's strength. A hand struck him in the eye, a boot hacked into his shin, a fist thumped low into his stomach. Silas fell to the ground. Viciously the older boy heaved the cart upside down and trampled its contents in the gutter.

"Let that teach you a lesson. Next time it'll be your face!"

With an angry laugh, for Silas had hurt him, Albert Dredge walked off.

"Rat's teeth! Sowface!" Silas shouted after him.

Slowly he crawled to his knees, then set the cart upright and collected his trampled goods. Limping, he continued homewards.

He did not whine or brood about what had occurred. Such incidents were common in the sprawling city.

By the time he reached the rag-and-bone yard night had fallen. Silas pushed his cart through the tall black gates, clashed them shut and dropped the locking bar in place. An oil lamp shone at the uncurtained window and cast fearsome shadows about the yard. There was a sound of voices. With a shout to show that he had returned, Silas hurried between the piles of junk.

The mermaid had woken. Prettily, though her forehead was gashed and her cheek scratched, she sat up against cushions with the blanket to her throat. On a chair at her side lay a mirror and hairbrush that had belonged to Silas's mother. There too lay the skeletons of two raw fish and a scatter of winkle shells.

"Looking better already, isn't she?" said his grand-father.

Grinning, Silas crossed the room.

The mermaid's hair, glossy as silk, trailed over the blanket. With clear eyes she regarded him. Silas looked down and was ashamed of his rags.

"Thank you for bringing me here. I think you saved my life." Her voice sounded of the sea – of wind and waves and the cry of birds. "Your grandfather too, he is very kind."

"He's the best," Silas said.

"He has given me all the food in your house."

Old Silas laughed. "And she's still hungry. What an appetite!" He pulled out two pennies. "Here, go round to Granny Porter's. Buy a couple of loaves."

"Is that what she wants – bread?"

"Fish!" the mermaid said promptly.

Silas looked at his grandfather. "I could take the boat out."

"Not tonight." The old man shook his head. "It's cold and windy. You've been out since before day-break."

"I'll be all right. I can stay inside the breakwater."

"No, boy," said his grandfather.

"Yes," said Silas. "Please, Granda. I can be back in an hour. Just let me get warmed up first. Then you can cook it and we'll all have a feast."

He limped to the fire.

"What have you done to yourself?"

"It's nothing." Silas stared into the flames. He would not tell his grandfather about the fight, he had too much to worry him already. "I tripped over, that's all."

"And hit your eye, I suppose."

"What do you mean?"

His grandfather handed him the mirror. Silas saw that his eye was crimson and purple.

"I banged it on the side of the cart," he said.

The mermaid had taken up the hairbrush. "When I am strong I will catch you lots of fish," she said.

Silas crouched at the hearth. Slowly the cold thawed from his bones. Then he pulled a set of crumpled oilskins from the beam, collected lantern, lines and bait, and started down the steep road to the harbour.

"Take care, boy." His grandfather called from the gate. "I don't like you fishing from the boat at night, especially in winter."

"Right, Granda." His voice drifted back through the gaslight and shadows.

Cold air swirled into the living-room. As she brush – brush – brushed her silken hair and gazed up at the forest of washing and implements that hung from the crooked beams, the mermaid crooned a low song.

In the middle of licking himself Sweep froze, listening

intently, and watched over his shoulder with eyes like yellow lamps.

Twenty minutes later Silas was rocking on black water inside the great breakwaters. Sheltering his tinder-box, he struck a spark and lit the storm lantern. Cheerily it swung above the peeling timbers. A stink of rotten fish and maggots rose from the bait tin as he prepared his line and cast it into the waves. A lead weight carried the hooks to the bottom; he pulled them back a little way. Then Silas hunched his shoulders against the wind, tugged the oilskin about his neck, and settled himself at the side of the boat. With one hand he jiggled the hooks up and down.

Shoals and solitary fish – harbour scavengers and some from the open sea – moved in the inky depths. They saw the flickering light on the surface and swam closer. With saucer eyes they regarded the teasing feathers and smelled the tantalizing bait. Round and round they circled, nuzzling the hooks. A big mouth opened.

The line twitched in Silas's fingers. He tugged sharply and felt the fish secure. Hand over hand he hauled the line aboard, dripping and icy cold. His fingernails ached. The fish, a strong codling, hung in the air. Silas caught it round the gills, pushed the hook free, and struck the fish's head on the seat beside him – two, three times. The fish leaped and shivered in a dying spasm. Silas dropped it at his feet and re-baited the hook.

In half an hour he caught five fish – another codling, an eel and two flounders. His thin shoulders shivered with the cold. Carefully he coiled the line, tidied the bottom of the boat, and took up the oars.

The current had carried him right to the harbour mouth. The lighthouse flashed fifty metres overhead. Briefly he looked round. Far out at sea a scatter of cargo ships rode at anchor; half a mile across the harbour the great steamers and sailing ships lay at their berths; lights glittered on the black water. Silas turned the *Sea Urchin*, pulled on the oars and made his way back to shore.

Halfway up the steep road from the quay, the gutted fish slung over his shoulder, he turned aside into a scrubbed passageway. Mouth-watering smells wafted from a bread oven. Granny Porter, an old woman with a clay pipe and several children sprawling about her feet, sold him two crusty loaves.

As he re-entered the house, Silas saw that everything was ready for the meal. His grandfather had been to the nearest inn and bought a jug of ale. The fire glowed red for cooking. A large frying pan lay in the hearth. He dropped the fish and loaves on the table and tugged off his oilskins.

A sharpened knife lay ready. Coughing, for the night air was bad for his chest, Old Silas caught hold of a codling, cut off its head and began to fillet the flesh from the bones.

"No!" The mermaid stretched out a taloned hand. "Give me one of the beardies now!"

Silas took the second codling to her on the settee. She snatched it and bit through the silver skin. Ravenously she munched and swallowed then bit again, showing the whites of her eyes. Silas watched with astonishment. By the time his grandfather set their own fish in the sizzling pan, the codling was finished. Delicately the mermaid laid the skeleton – head at one end, tail at the other – on the chair beside her and sucked her fingers clean.

The grandfather clock struck nine.

Still cold from the night, Silas crouched close to the fire and hung a slice of bread on a toasting fork. The fish spat in the soot-blackened pan, savoury blue smoke rose into the room. His grandfather poured three mugs of ale. Silas quenched the foam with his lips and watched as the old man carried one to the settee.

The mermaid did not respond. Her head had fallen sideways upon the cushions, her wild eyes were closed. Once more she was sound asleep.

Chapter Four

Ooli

"The Islands of the Sun," Silas said.

"Beyond the horizon, far away," said the mermaid. "Where the wind blows warm and the waves are full of dolphins."

"Oh, it sounds a fine place!"

It was midday. Silas had been out with the cart all morning, delivering a load of bones to the glue factory up-river. Now he sat on the worn rug near the fire and curled bare feet beneath him. A violent shower rattled on the window.

"Full of dolphins," he repeated. "Go on, what else?"

The mermaid sat against the cushions and took Sweep on to her lap. The little cat rolled on its back as she tickled it beneath the chin.

"What will I tell you? The seas are blue and green. Waves break on bright sands and the rocks are full of wild flowers." She smiled at the memory. "All day long the sun shines, and at night the stars are clear. There are palm trees and fresh waterfalls. Groves of orange and other fruit grow close to the shore. The water is warm and the sun strikes deep. There are sea forests and giant clams, oysters with pearls as big as a seagull's egg."

"It sounds beautiful," Silas said. "Eh, Granda?"

"Indeed it does." Old Silas struggled with a cough and put a hand to his chest.

"If we were there you'd get strong again, wouldn't you."

"If we were there, boy. If pigs could fly. It's a long way from the city."

Silas turned back to the mermaid. "But if you live in those sunny islands what are you doing here? The water's cold and grey; we have winter storms."

"Every mermaid – of my tribe – has to make a journey," she said.

"And you came to Britain?"

"I have travelled round the world." She pulled her fingers from Sweep's playful claws.

"Around the world!" Silas echoed. "My father travelled around the world. He was a sailor." He crossed to the dresser and handed her a small portrait in a cheap wooden frame. It was his most treasured possession. "That's my dad."

The portrait had been painted by one of his father's

shipmates. The mermaid examined it closely.

"He has a brave face," she said. "He looks like you."

"Mm." Silas examined the picture afresh, dusted it carefully with his ragged sleeve and returned it to the dresser.

"Where is your father now?" said the mermaid.

"He died," Silas said briefly.

"His ship never came back," said his grandfather.

"How did you travel," Silas changed the subject, "when you went round the world?"

"How do you think?" She smiled. "I swam."

As she lay on the old settee it was hard to believe. Her brow was cut and her shoulder bruised. She seemed too young and frail.

"It has been a long journey." Taking up the brush she drew it through her hair. "And it is not finished yet. Many mermaids never return to the islands. I may not myself."

"I bet you've had lots of adventures."

"Yes, there are stories to tell." She retraced her journey. "I have chased shoals of penguins beneath the floating ice-mountains of the south; ridden whales in the jade-green seas of the equator. I have teased the great white shark and appeared to eskimos through holes in the ice; lain warm beside polar bears on the ice-lilies of the arctic sea."

"Oh!" Silas said again and his face shone.

"But what are you doing here?" Old Silas repeated the question. "Washed up on the shore and hiding among seaweed?"

"Far in the north where the winter days are dark," said the mermaid, "I made a roaring storm. For days I followed it south, riding the waves and whipping them higher, laughing as the ships ran for shelter. It was wonderful but I grew tired. For one moment I was careless ... the rest you know."

Silas stared. "You mean *you* made that storm?"

"My people have that power." She shrugged and took up the mirror.

"Is it true what they say, that mermaids sit on dangerous rocks and tempt sailors to their death by singing?"

"Some mermaids, yes, but we are not all alike. There are many tribes of mermaids – as there are many tribes of people and fish and birds. My grandfather – like your father – was a sailor from England. His boat was wrecked in the Islands of the Sun. We are a happy people. But a hundred miles away there is a savage race whose eyes are red. In their underwater palaces the roofs are supported by the skeletons of drowned men, one above the other, with weed for hair and crabs in their mouths. In their horrid gardens the souls of sailors are caged with sharks and giant octopuses. We call their land the Islands of Bones."

A heavy down-draught puffed smoke from the fire.

"Other mermaids," she continued, "dare not leave the sea, for in air they turn to water. And far to the west there is a tribe whose people are so large that each finger is longer than your tallest man; any ship that sails into their floating hair is trapped and the sailors are devoured."

Silas's imagination ran riot. For a time he was silent then he said, "Tell me your name again."

"Luiulia," she said, her voice like running water.

"Looi-oolia," Silas said with difficulty. "Luiulia. It's hard to say."

"For you, perhaps. On land I am sometimes called Ooli." She set the brush and mirror aside and looked hopefully towards the table. "Is there any fish left?"

"No," said Old Silas. "You ate the last one an hour ago."

The rain had stopped, a shaft of thin sunshine struck the scrapyard.

"It's all right," said Silas. "I'm just going out fishing now."

He pulled on his cracked boots and reached for the oilskins.

"You are both very kind," the mermaid said for the twentieth time. "When I am strong again I will try to reward you."

"There's no need for that," said Old Silas.

"I'll be back before dark." Silas dropped his tackle into a bucket and prepared to leave. "Bye, Granda. Bye, Luiulia – Ooli."

A cold gust blew from the rag-and-bone yard. With a businesslike bang the door shut behind him.

Ooli recovered quickly. Her scars began to heal, the bruises faded. On hands and silver tail she hauled herself about the splintery floor and looked from the window.

A large wooden barrel stood at one side of the yard, gathering rainwater from the roof. It was the height of a man's chest and brim-full.

For a long time Ooli regarded this. Her tail was itchy from being so long out of water. Vigorously she scratched, scattering the floor with scales like mother-of-pearl.

"If I go outside," she said on the fourth morning of her stay, "will you help me into the barrel?"

Silas stood at the door shaking her blanket. Long hairs and a shower of large scales whirled up on the wind.

"It's cold," he said. "Look."

The sides of the barrel were crusted with ice. Thin drifts of hail lay in corners of the yard.

"The water will be freezing!"

"That makes no difference." She laughed. "Warm is best but mermaids don't feel the cold the same as you."

Silas ran to make sure the gates were locked, then with

her seal-like gait Ooli crawled down the yard. The wind blew the surface of the barrel into a miniature sea. Silas and his grandfather lifted her, dodging aside as her long tail slid into the water and waves cascaded about their trousers.

"Ohhhhh!" The mermaid ducked from sight and wriggled in an ecstasy of pleasure. "Lovely!" With both hands she drew a tangle of hair from her shoulders and ducked again. "Ohhhh! To feel clean again!"

"But aren't you cold at all?" Silas blew on his fingers.

"Wonderful!" She laughed and flung a scatter of water at his face.

"I'm going inside." Old Silas coughed and gripped the collar of his jacket. "Give me a shout when you want to come out again." Hunch-shouldered, he returned to the house.

Ten minutes later Silas joined him at the fire. Steam rose from their wet trousers. Out in the yard the mermaid sang softly – beautiful unearthly songs that made shivers run up and down Silas's spine.

"You'd better tell her to be quiet," said his grandfather. "If she keeps singing like that, someone's going to climb up and look over the wall."

But Ooli herself realized the danger and a moment later the singing stopped.

"Silas," came her voice from the yard. "Will you bring me the comb and mirror."

For an hour she remained in the rainwater barrel, happily combing her hair and considering her reflection, sloshing her tail from side to side, and every few minutes, unable to prevent herself, breaking into snatches of song.

When the coast was clear, Silas ran out into the street to fill buckets at the pump, and tipped the icy streams over her delighted head.

The routine of the house was disturbed. At dawn each morning Silas went fishing. This made him late to start work, so his rounds were not finished until long after sunset. On blistered and chilblained feet he scoured the city for scrap, and when he had gathered a load he delivered it to dealers. Tired in the evenings, he sat by the fire with his grandfather and the mermaid, and swapped tales of the teeming city for tales of the sea.

Old Silas told bloodcurdling stories of robbery and murder. Many of these took place in the *Alleys*, a fearful part of the city inhabited by villains and ruffians. Policemen and excisemen dared not enter those twisted lanes, and many innocents who wandered in by mistake were never seen again. At the heart of the Alleys, in Hangman Square, stood the *Black Parrot*, a notorious inn. Old Silas was a good storyteller. His tales of what went on there at night made his grandson and the little mermaid shiver and look behind them at the shadows cast by the firelight and flickering candle flame.

Silas, for his part, told Ooli of his adventures with the rag-cart, and confessed his recent trouble with Jasper and Albert Dredge. He recounted how father and son wandered the city, bullying and burgling, shoplifting and picking pockets, always on the lookout for a dishonest penny. They were mixed up with a gang from the Alleys – indeed some said that Jasper was landlord of the *Black Parrot*. A dozen times he had been arrested, and every time freed from jail by a band of desperadoes.

But most of their tales were happier, many made them laugh. And Ooli added stories of shipwreck and pirates, monsters and drowned cities, the Islands of Bones and the Islands of the Sun – stories like a breath of wind from the high seas.

Every morning Silas planned to go to bed early, and every evening he sat up beyond midnight, unwilling to leave the fire and company, even though his eyes were ringed with tiredness.

"Tomorrow," Ooli announced one evening, a week or so after her arrival, "you must row your boat to a quiet part of the shore. Then carry me down on the cart. Together we will go far out to sea and I shall catch you a large haul of fish."

"You're not going away!" Silas dreaded the day when

his new-found friend would swim off and he would never see her again. "Not yet. Stay a while longer."

"No, I am not leaving. I am happy here, it is an adventure." Her eyes sparkled. "But I must swim again and dive. At the same time, perhaps, I can repay you a little for your kindness."

And so, while it was still dark the following morning, Silas pulled his boat from its mooring and rowed out into the middle of the sleeping harbour. When he was well clear of the big ships with their ropes and anchors, he hoisted his small sail, took the tiller, and sailed out between the tremendous breakwaters. The *Sea Urchin* bounced on the waves of the open sea. Silas steered a short distance along the coast and tied up at a quiet gully in the rocks.

In the first glimmer of dawn he returned along the empty streets to the rag-and-bone yard. His grandfather had the cart scrubbed clean and ready. Together they helped Ooli to climb up, and covered her with rags. Then Silas started back to the beach.

In half an hour he reached the far end of the lower promenade and pushed the cart over bumpy rocks, as close to the *Sea Urchin* as possible. Carefully he looked up and down the shore. Except for a distant kelp-gatherer and a far-off figure on the cliff-top, it was deserted. Quickly he tipped the cart and helped Ooli to the ground. Like an eel she slithered across pebbles and weedy rocks towards the gully, uttering little cries as she went, and without a backward glance slipped headfirst into the black and silver water. There was scarcely a splash. The narrow channel was very deep.

Silas waited but the mermaid did not reappear. A minute passed. He ran to the water's edge and scanned the rocks. A second minute slipped by.

"Silas!" A laughing head regarded him from a patch of weed almost at his feet. "Here." Reaching up, she handed him a gigantic lobster, bright blue and as fresh as the morning. "Put it in the boat," she cried. "Quickly! Quickly! I want to swim!"

Neat as a dolphin she sprang from the water and disappeared in a perfect dive.

Silas hurried to the rocking *Sea Urchin* and put the lobster in a fish box, then cast off and took the oars. Soon he was fifty metres from shore and set the patched red sail. The wind blew it full. Side by side the grubby rag-and-bone boy and the dancing mermaid headed out to sea.

As the early sun, dazzling and orange, broke through cloud, they were two miles from land. At their backs the great city had shrunk to a line along the horizon. Toy factory chimneys released plumes of smoke into the dirty air. Hills, never seen from the busy streets, rose above the steeples. Ships moved in and out of harbour on the morning tide.

The *Sea Urchin* pitched and rolled on waves that swept in from the open sea. It was exciting and a little frightening. Silas had never been so far out by himself.

The lobster had escaped from its box and crawled about in the bottom of the boat, snapping its tail and waving its claws. Carefully Silas recaptured it. As he did so, Ooli emerged from the water in a shower of spray. One hand caught the bow, the other gripped a bright mackerel. Neatly she nipped it across the back of the head with her teeth and tossed it into the boat.

"You like the blue darters? They sell well?"

"Yes."

"There is a big shoal. Give me a string."

Silas cut a length of fishing line. With a laugh Ooli took it and let go of the bow. Her long tail swept. Like an arrow she pierced the heart of a glassy wave, sprang into the air and was gone.

The boy waited, staring into the water. He began to feel anxious – how could she be gone for so long? Then something silver glimmered in the depths, far beneath him. Rapidly it rose. In another bright scatter of spray the mermaid burst into the sunlight. In the same movement she slung a string of fish aboard. Ten mackerel were threaded through their mouths and gills.

"Give me another string," she cried. "I will catch you thirty and then go deep for the silver beardies."

Despite the cold her skin was pink and fresh. Like silken weed her long hair floated in the waves.

In an hour the boat was loaded. Cod and mottled blue mackerel, haddock and red-spotted plaice, spilled from the overflowing box and slithered around the bottom of the boat. Lobsters and big pink crabs clambered from bow to stern.

"No more! That's enough!" Silas laughed and dodged a determined set of claws.

"Good." Ooli hung from the side. "You will sell them to make much money. Now come. Look." She pointed to an island a mile further out. It was deserted. Towering cliffs plunged into the sea. "There is a cave. Follow me."

With a flick of her tail she swam ahead and waited, bobbing in the swell, while Silas set his red sail and took his place at the tiller. Steadily the *Sea Urchin* ploughed a track across the sea while the mermaid played in the dancing waves.

As the cliffs drew closer a thousand seabirds wheeled overhead. The air was loud with their clamour. Throwing back her head, Ooli imitated their cries and they swooped to investigate. White wings rushed about the boat.

The cave was enormous and filled with rocking water. A small beach lay to one side, sunlit and sheltered from the November wind. Silas lowered his sail and rowed between barnacle-covered rocks. Long weed swirled beneath him. The bows of the *Sea Urchin* drove up on pebbles. He took off his boots and sprang overboard into the shallow water. As he tied up the boat, Ooli slid from the sea beside him.

"Let us make a fire," she said. "Look, there is dry grass and driftwood caught in the rocks."

Silas broke the wood and built a little tent of sticks and grass, then struck a spark from his tinder-box. Soon a hot fire spat and flared in a hollow of the rocks. With his knife he cleaned two fish and set them on twigs to bake. His mouth watered as the skin crackled and a succulent scent mingled with the woodsmoke. Ooli, as always, preferred her fish raw. She cracked a handful of blue mussels, like nuts, on a smooth stone. Side by side Silas and the mermaid toasted their faces at the flames.

It was late afternoon as the *Sea Urchin* headed homeward to the gully in the rocks. Daylight faded, red and bruised above the smoky city. The beach was nearly empty. Silas transferred the fish to his cart and wrapped the crabs and lobsters in wet rags so that they could not nip. Then he moored the boat securely for the night and hid Ooli beside his load.

It was a struggle to haul the cart up the rocks but he managed and was soon rattling on the road home – along the promenade, up past the fishermen's cottages, and into the warren of streets with their lamplit inns.

His cheeks glowed from the sun and salt wind.

Chapter Five

Fog

"Fresh fish!" Silas cried shrilly in the crowded streets. "Mackerel! Haddock! Live crabs and lobsters! Buy your fresh fish here!"

It was a bright morning. Silas had scrubbed his hands and face in the yard and wrapped an old tablecloth round his waist for an apron. Cautious wives and cooks from the big houses leaned over his cart and turned the fish with their pink fingers. Long noses sniffed suspiciously.

"Caught last night," Silas assured them jauntily. "Fresh from the salt sea."

"What's this 'ere?" A stout mother pointed to a little semi-circle of teeth marks.

"Just a mark from the net," Silas said. "Nothin' to worry about, Ma. Look, this one's the same."

"Looks like someone's been biting 'em," she said.

But she bought. Silas wrapped the fish in a sheet of newspaper and pocketed the coins she dropped into his palm.

"Be comin' regular, will you?" she said.

"I hope so," Silas answered.

"See you again, then." She hurried off, two children clinging to her coat.

"Codling! Eels! Buy your fresh fish here!"

The cart was soon half empty.

In the busy street Silas took no notice of footsteps at his back. A hand grasped his arm. Thick fingers dug into his muscle.

"Silas Fisher again!"

It was Jasper Dredge. Before Silas could move, a big fist clumped him across the ear.

"That's for chuckin' stones," he heard dimly through the ringing in his head. "Next time I'll take my belt to you. An' you'd better remember that, you little 'ooligan."

Albert was with him. He smiled, revealing his yellow rat's teeth. "Look, Pa. He's changed his trade. Fishmonger now, he is."

"Very nice, an' all." Jasper looked the cart over. His belly hung above the top of his trousers.

With a fat hand Albert took a large plaice, dropped it in the gutter, and screwed it into a mess with his boot.

"Less o' that, Albert," said his father. "Don't want to spoil your stock, do you?"

"Why, Pa, you don't mean – " Albert's mouth opened in a leer of understanding. "Oh, that's ripe, that is. That's rich! You're the one, Pa."

"Understand, do you?" Smelling like a pole-cat, Jasper crowded Silas against an iron railing. "I want to borrow your cart, all right? Call at the *Black Parrot* tomorrow mornin' – if you dare – an' maybe I'll tell you where to pick it up."

Albert seized the cart by the handles and prepared to push it away.

"Get off! Let go of that!" Silas struggled helplessly. "That's my cart! Them's my fish!"

Jasper's grip tightened on the neck of Silas's jacket. His beard thrust into the boy's face. "If I was you I'd keep me trap shut. See this?" He touched a big sheath-knife that hung on his belt.

Silas rolled his eyes down.

"One more squeak out o' you an' next time we meet I'll slit your gizzard! Understand? Cut your tripes out!"

Scarcely able to breathe, Silas nodded.

"I understand an' all." A young costermonger had left his fruit stall and tapped Jasper Dredge on the shoulder. With a strong hand he broke the grip on Silas's collar. "If there's one thing I can't stand, it's someone that bullies little kids."

"You keep your nose out o' this," Jasper blustered. "Stole them from my boy, he did. The little rat's a thief."

"I did not!" Silas cried.

"A liar an' all!" Jasper exclaimed. "So don't stick your face into things you know nothin' about – right?" Roughly he pushed the costermonger aside.

"I'll tell you one more time," the costermonger said. "Leave the kid alone. Them's his fish. Here, you, fatty!" He called to Albert. "Fetch that cart back 'ere."

Flaring up in anger, Jasper swung a punch while the man's back was turned. It struck the young costermonger on the back of the head. But he was sturdy. In an instant he turned, and before Jasper could move, a hard fist struck him right on the nose. With a howl of pain – for like most bullies Jasper Dredge was also a coward – he fell backwards to the kerb and put a hand to the blood that streamed from his nostrils.

The costermonger ignored him and put an arm around Silas's shoulders. "All right, son?"

He nodded.

"Best be on your way, then. If red-whiskers here bothers you again, you let me know."

"Thanks."

Silas grasped the handles of his cart and headed away through the crowd. His heart was thudding. He did not see Albert Dredge on the opposite side of the street – fat

Albert, thick-lipped and shifty-eyed – who dodged from doorway to doorway and kept pace alongside as he continued through the heart of the city.

By midday the last fish was sold, the last snapping lobster transferred from box to shopping basket. The encounter with Jasper Dredge half-forgotten, Silas set off homeward through the crowded streets. His heart was light, his pocket heavy with coins – more than a fortnight's takings in a single morning. His cart bounced cheerfully on the cobbles.

In less than an hour he was back at the rag-and-bone yard. With a carefree crash he slammed the gates and let himself into the house.

Fifty metres distant, Albert Dredge watched from a shadowy entrance. There had been no chance in the midday streets of catching Silas and giving him the drubbing Albert thought he so richly deserved – and Albert was certainly not running the risk of a punch on the nose like his father. Ever watchful, he sidled along the wall and put an eye to a crack in the gates. Nothing was to be seen but the empty cart and piles of junk. Tentatively he pushed but the gate was barred. He looked up. An active boy, an athletic boy, could have climbed the wall – but not Albert Dredge.

Yet if Albert was fat and cowardly, he was also patient. Furtively he looked up and down the street and selected a corner out of the wind. He wanted to know where a rag-and-bone boy had got hold of all that fish. There was money to be made – good money. He had made sure where Silas lived. Now it was simply a matter of waiting. From a tight pocket he unearthed a fragment of toffee. Then, tucking plump knees to his chest, he settled himself in the thin November sunshine.

Early the following morning Silas left the rag-and-bone yard with the mermaid hidden beneath her covering of rags. The air was still, a halo of mist hung about the gas lamps. Fat drips fell in the silence.

They reached the promenade high above the sea; rattled down to the lower promenade; continued to the far end; and crossed the deserted shore to the *Sea Urchin*, rocking safely at her mooring. At once Ooli slid from the cart and hauled herself across the weedy rocks. Neat as an otter she slipped into the gully. Silas stepped aboard his boat and prepared to row out into the dove-grey sea.

Half an hour after Silas had departed, Albert Dredge arrived at the rag-and-bone yard. He had stayed until long after dark the previous night and came back early – but not early enough, for the gates were unlocked. Cautiously he pushed one ajar and looked into the yard. A black kitten scampered away. The cart had gone. Albert swore for it had been a walk of three miles on a chill morning. Moreover, he had eaten no breakfast. He glared around. An elderly lamplighter moved up the street towards him, extinguishing gaslights in the leaden gleam of dawn.

"Hey," Albert called. "Have you seen a boy with a cart?"

The lamplighter did not like his tone. "I might 'ave," he answered.

"The boy from the rag-yard there."

"I can't quite remember." The lamplighter spat and looked pointedly at his hand.

"Oh!" Albert felt in his pocket and pulled out a halfpenny. Grudgingly he laid it in the grimy palm.

"Threepence," the lamplighter said. "Albert Dredge, isn't it? You can afford it."

"Robber!" Albert pulled out three more coins.

The lamplighter chuckled and tucked the money away. "Young Silas Fisher? Yes, I saw 'im 'eading down to the shore. 'Bout 'alf an hour ago. Pile o' rags on the back of 'is cart."

"Thanks!" Albert said sarcastically. Abruptly he seized the lamplighter's pole, snapped the top beneath his foot and flung the hook away over the roofs. There was a crash of glass. "That'll teach you to play games with the Dredges!" He ran off along the street.

Albert did not run far for his fat shook at every stride. Slowing to a walk, he pressed on. Soon he came to the sea. Albert did not like the sea. Panting, he grasped the rail of the upper promenade and surveyed the beach. Nothing moved except the glassy waves. Beyond the breakwaters, almost hidden by the gathering mist, great ships hung at anchor, waiting for the morning tide. He strained his eyes. A short distance along the coast a small boat headed out from the rocks. A single figure pulled on the oars. Albert let go of the rail and hurried on along the promenade.

Silas's cart stood on the rocks, a jumble of rags held down by stones. Of the boat there was no sign. Albert stared out to sea. White walls of mist drifted above the water.

It was going to be a long cold wait. Already his hair was damp. Albert hunted on the cart for some clean rags and draped them around his shoulders. Then pulling his collar close, he felt in his pocket for a slice of pork pie and settled in the shelter of a rock.

Far out at sea the mist was magical. Closer and closer it pressed about the boat. Invisible steamers hooted like forlorn ghosts. Silas shipped his oars. The red sail hung motionless.

With a scatter of icy drops Ooli burst from the sea. Gaily she romped about the boat.

"You're sure you know the way back?" Silas called.

The mermaid laughed and pointed, spinning on her

tail. "The lighthouse – the gully – the cave – the open sea. Oh!" Suddenly she was still. "I feel something – the Grey Brothers!"

With a leap and a dive she was gone.

Silas waited. He had grown used to her long absences. Two minutes passed – three.

Suddenly Silas sensed that he was not alone. He felt eyes upon him and stared on all sides into the mist. A dark shape had appeared on the rocking sea. He saw another – they were seals. Soon all about the boat the water was filled with dark heads and bristling whiskers. Gentle eyes stared towards him.

Ooli broke surface and hooked an arm over the boat's side. "The Grey Brothers," she laughed. "They will fish for you. And the Merrifins too. They are not far away." Throwing back her head she called aloud: "Paloo! Paloo!" In the middle of each cry she plunged her mouth into the water. "Paloo! Palooooo!"

In the silence they waited. Then there was a noise of distant splashing and a school of porpoises appeared through the mist, speeding and springing from the glassy waves.

"Come, we will fish!" Luiulia whistled three times, then cried loudly in a strange tongue and pointed to the boat.

The porpoises scattered, lively as a flock of birds, and in a moment the seals too were gone. Some sank without trace, others rolled and dived, sleek on the surface of the sea.

All at once Silas was alone. He stared down into the water and out into the walls of white mist.

With no warning the boat rocked violently as a seal shot into the air, right alongside. In its jaws was a huge cod, a fish half as long as Silas himself. With a toss of the head it flung the fish into the boat and crashed back into the sea.

Silas had scarcely recovered his balance when a porpoise leaped up on the other side, and another at the bows. Giant fish flew about him.

The boat tossed wildly as in a storm – stem to stern, port to starboard. It was lucky Silas wore his oilskins for spray drenched him from head to foot as the seals and porpoises sprang up on every side.

A big haddock struck him full in the middle. "Ooofff!" Silas doubled up and fell to the bottom-boards. Fish slithered about his face. A conger eel well over a metre long began to wriggle up his trouser leg. As soon as he had recovered his breath, he scrambled to his knees and began raking the catch into order.

Soon the boat was full, so full that many more fish must put it in danger of sinking.

Ooli, who had joined the Grey Brothers and Merrifins in their orgy of fishing, clung to the bow and called to each as it flung its catch into the boat. Gradually the storm of fish slackened. A last halibut and mackerel slithered across the seat and struck Silas's leg.

"Pass me the mooring line," Ooli called.

Silas groped beneath fish for the rope and doubled it as she instructed him. Neatly he fastened the middle to a ringbolt in the prow of the boat and passed the ends over the side. Ooli tied a noose in each and slipped them over the heads of two large seals.

"Swim, Grey Brothers." She pointed. "To the great cave in the island. There are no hunters in the mist, you will be safe."

The seals tugged the bow-rope. Slowly at first, then faster, the *Sea Urchin* slid through the waves. On every side the sea was alive with sleek bodies, leaping and diving. Seabirds flew overhead. Hardly seeming to move her tail, the little mermaid kept pace beside the towing seals.

Silas looked round him with delight. The cargo of fish slithered about his legs. Tucking his hands into wet pockets he listened to the water hissing past the bow, and peered ahead into the mist for the first glimpse of the island.

Fortunately his tinder box had remained dry and soon he crouched beside a spitting fire on the pebbly beach near the cave. All about him lay the seals, waving their flippers, dozing and watching with round watery eyes. Porpoises drifted in the deep water of the cave entrance.

Ooli tickled one of the seals under the chin and murmured softly.

Silas turned his roasting fish and held red hands to the flames. He had spread his oilskins on a nearby rock. His boots hung upside down on sticks thrust into the pebbles.

An hour slipped by. Steadily the fog thickened. In the silence the waves splashed musically about the rocks and lapped the timbers of the little boat. A few seagulls bobbed on the tide, cormorants spread their wings to dry. To Silas, a rag-and-bone boy from the city, it was as if he was the only person left alive in a strange world.

Ooli joined him beside the fire. Eating with fingers, he pulled a roast mackerel to pieces and popped them into his mouth, burning hot.

He was idyllically happy.

Albert Dredge, meanwhile, had also made a fire, a short distance from the rag-cart. It was cold on the November shore. To his dismay, as he held podgy hands towards the heat, he was joined by a straggle of winkle-gatherers – first one, then another – bent old crones like witches, ancient men in ragged coats. Albert did not like their company, did not want them near when the boat returned. Rising impatiently, he kicked the blazing sticks into a pool and stamped on what remained. The winkle-gatherers cried angrily. One ran at him with clawed hands. Then they went away and Albert was left alone above the slurping gully. His mean eyes scanned the mist for signs of the returning boat.

But what, he began to wonder, if the ragboy was not alone – for his glimpse of the boat had not been clear. Had there been a second figure – or was it a mast? What if some of the ghastly winkle-gatherers or a sailor were nearby when Silas came ashore? Albert began to wish that his father was with him. After a time he made his way back to the promenade and fishermen's cottages above the beach.

"Hey!" Hidden from the cottage windows he seized a younger boy by the jacket. "Do you want to earn twopence?"

"Doin' what?" The boy wriggled in his grasp.

"Go a message for me."

"All right." The boy took the two pennies. "Where to?"

"You heard o' the *Black Parrot*?"

"What! In the Alleys! I ain't goin' to the *Black Parrot*!"

Albert caught the boy's wrist and twisted his arm up his back.

"It's miles away!" the boy protested. "My dad wouldn't let me. It's full of thieves an' murderers! Kids disappear!"

"You took the money," Albert said. "It's a deal."

"Ow!" The boy shouted as Albert screwed his arm up between his shoulders.

"An' there'll be a penny more when you come back – that's if you keep your trap shut. If you don't," Albert smiled with dirty teeth, "I'll break your arm. If you make it so I 'ave to go myself, I'll bring some o' them cut-throats back with me. One night when it's good an' dark we'll come an' look you up!"

"You don't know which is my 'ouse."

"There's ways of finding out everything. You should see their ropes – an' razors!" He gave the arm a wrench.

"All right! I'll go!"

"An' tell nobody?"

"No!"

"That's better." Albert eased the pressure. "Now, you go to the *Black Parrot* – quick, mind – an' ask for Jasper Dredge. Tell him that Albert says he's to come down here, right away. An' tell him he'd better bring Bosun – that's his dog – he might be needed. Got that?"

The boy nodded. Tears ran down his cheeks.

"An' he's to bring some grub with him. Now, repeat the message."

The boy did so.

"Right, then, off you go. An' no tricks!"

Albert pushed him away. The boy stumbled and fell headlong, then scrambled to his feet and ran away up the twisting road.

Albert sniggered. "I keep thinkin' about them cut-throats," he called loudly. "You'd better be quick!"

Soon the boy was swallowed up in the mist. Cheered by the encounter, Albert returned to his seat on the rocks.

Weed, like dark hair, trailed backwards and forwards in the gully. The mist was thickening all the time. It was going to be a real pea-souper.

Chapter Six

The *Morning Star*

"Goodbye!" Silas waved as the whiskery seals and leaping porpoises circled the boat and headed back to sea. "Goodbye!"

It was late afternoon. The fog was now very dense indeed. There was no reddening of the sky, no sunset. The walls of mist that pressed about the boat turned from pearl to grey, darkening above the black and pewter sea.

In moments the Grey Brothers and Merrifins were gone. Silas pulled the towing-lines aboard and took the oars. The cargo of fish slithered about his legs.

"This way." Ooli's eyes were bright. She had enjoyed the day with Silas and her sea companions.

There was little need for directions for the seals had towed the boat so close to shore that the splash of waves rose through the mist.

Silas pulled gently; he did not wish to run the *Sea*

Urchin on to the rocks.

"To the right," called Ooli.

Dimly through the mist Silas found himself drifting into the mouth of the deep gully. It was too narrow to row. He stood and sculled with a single oar over the stern. The boat rocked forward and soon reached the spot where he would off-load the fish. Silas sprang ashore and looped the painter round a point of rock.

He did not see Albert Dredge and his father peering from their hiding place, nor the ugly yellow mongrel that shivered at Jasper's feet. Their eyes were full of wonder at the pretty mermaid who swam at the boy's side and hauled herself into the fish-laden boat.

Silas scrambled over the rocks to his cart. He threw the stones from the rags and pulled the cart as close to the gully as possible.

"I can't carry it all in one load," he called to Ooli. "I'll take you and some of the fish first, then come back for the rest. Perhaps I can borrow the horse and cart from Granny Porter. I've never seen such a catch!"

The mermaid was pleased and began heaving the heavy fish on to the rocks. Silas collected them, fingers through the gills, and stacked them head-to-tail on the cart.

"That's enough," he called ten minutes later. "The rest should be safe until I come back. Everybody'll have gone home by now."

He began to drag the loaded cart up the shore. Ooli slid from the boat on to the weedy rocks and crawled alongside.

As soon as they were safely clear of the water, Jasper Dredge and Albert sprang from their hiding place and rushed forward through the fog. Silas and Ooli were taken completely by surprise. There was a brief but fierce and noisy struggle. Silas kicked and struck out but he was no match for fat Albert and soon lay pinned among weed and fish with the older boy on top of him. Luiulia fought like a wild thing. Her talons pierced Jasper's jacket and tore his arm. She struck at his face and pummelled his chest, but on land she was half helpless. Bosun darted from his master's feet, snarling and snapping. With a big fist Jasper knocked the mermaid across the pebbles. Hastily, to avoid those claws, he seized a bundle of rags and flung them over her head and shoulders. Roughly he bound them about her waist and tugged the knots tight.

A child on the promenade and the last of the stooped winkle-gatherers heard the cries and shouts – but in those days many things happened that it was safer to ignore. Hidden by the thick fog, they hurried off in the opposite direction.

"What are we goin' to do with 'im, Pa?" Albert screwed a knuckle into Silas's back and grinned.

"You decide, son." Jasper sucked blood from the

back of his hand. "What do you want to do with 'im?"

"Tie a rock to 'is feet an' drop 'im in the water," Albert said eagerly.

"You'll end up with a rope around your neck!" his father commented. "No need for that – not yet, anyway. But if he gives us any more trouble we might think about it."

"Heh-heh, that's good! D'you 'ear that?" Albert forced Silas's face into the weed and looked up at his father. "What, then, Pa?"

Jasper scratched his red beard. "I know. Bring him down to the boat."

Leaving Ooli helpless, father and son dragged Silas back to the gully.

"You get in the boat," Jasper said to Albert. "Chuck the oars an' mast over the side. The sail an' all."

Readily Albert did so. Anything destructive gave him pleasure.

"Now untie that rope an' throw it up 'ere. Keep 'old o' the rock, you fool!"

Jasper cut two lengths from the mooring line. Tightly he bound Silas's hands and feet. The rough rope cut into his bones. He thrust a ball of rag into his mouth and gagged him. With rough hands he went through his pockets. Silas's knife and other few possessions vanished into the water. Then taking the boy by his collar and the seat of his ragged trousers, Jasper pitched him headfirst into the boat.

It was a drop of several feet. Luckily his fall was broken by fish. Winded, Silas lay among the haddock and cod.

"Right, Albert, you come out," Jasper said.

"But what about all them fish, Pa?" Albert scrambled to the rocks. "They're worth quids!"

"Use your loaf, son. Chicken feed compared with 'er up there. 'Sides, you want to push that cart all the way to 'Angman Square – two, three times?"

With an end of rope Jasper towed the little boat to the mouth of the gully. Setting his foot on the stern, he gave it a hard push into deep water.

Albert sniggered at his side.

"Tide flows out to sea from 'ere," Jasper said, "straight to the 'orizon. By the time the fog lifts he'll be out of sight o' land." He called aloud to Silas. "'Ear that, young Fisher? I've give you a chance. You get out o' this alive an' get in my way again, I'll cut your liver out an' fry it for breakfast. An' you'd better remember that!"

Albert picked some stones from a pool and flung them after the boat that drifted out from shore. Muffled noises came from Silas's gag; they saw him struggling and falling among the fish. The boat rocked violently. At length he managed to sit on a seat, a desolate figure in the gathering darkness. A stone thudded among the fish, another splashed alongside. And a minute later the *Sea Urchin* had disappeared into the fog.

Jasper Dredge and Albert returned to the cart.

"May as well keep the fish we've got." Jasper began collecting them from the rocks.

"A mermaid!" Albert poked at the tail that emerged from Ooli's smothering rags. "That's some catch, Pa, eh? What are we going to do with 'er?"

"What do you think!" his father said. "Show her, o' course. There's money to be made – big money! But first we take 'er back to the *Black Parrot*."

The cart was set on its wheels. Ooli lashed out blindly with her tail. Jasper threw a noose round the end and tied it to her neck. Roughly they flung her on the cart and heaped the fish after.

"An' remember this," Jasper threatened. "You make a sound an' you'll feel the weight o' my fist. You 'ear?"

The mermaid was silent.

They threw the rest of the rags on top and secured them with Silas's ropes. Together they heaved the cart up the shore. Then Jasper and Albert set off for the *Black Parrot* in Hangman Square – miles from the sea, in the heart of the wicked Alleys.

The streets were eerie and unfamiliar with fog. Light from the gas-lamps struggled to the ground.

As the wheels rattled over the cobblestones, Ooli shook with sobs. Of all things in the world, imprisonment was the one she feared most. Cut off from the sea, her freedom lost, she was sure she would die.

Silas stared around into the shrouding mist. It was hard to say how far he had drifted but he thought quite a distance for the waves were higher. He was frightened and very cold. Coughing, he pushed with his tongue at the choking gag. For the hundredth time he struggled with his feet and strained at the rope that bound his thin wrists. His skin was raw but still the knots held tight.

It was total night. On all sides, far and near, came the dismal hoots of ships inching through the fog, and bells from those at anchor.

An hour passed.

The cold black bottomless water glinted under the bows. Silas shuddered and pulled his chin down into his oilskins.

Another hour.

The bells and foghorns began to recede. In his imagination Silas saw himself drifting out of sight of land, saw the waves of the open sea toss him high on their crests. He tried not to panic and listened to the ghostly sounds.

Gradually he became aware that one sound was growing louder. He strained his ears and heard the low throb of a ship's engine. The bray of the foghorn drew closer – and closer. Silas stared into the fog.

In the darkness he never saw the ship until suddenly, with a bump, something struck his boat and sent him tumbling among the fish. He gazed up and saw a black cliff towering overhead. Slowly it slid past, scraping the side of the boat and spinning it round. Desperately Silas tried to shout. The ball of cloth in his mouth began to unravel and slip down his throat. He rolled on his face and coughed helplessly.

But overhead a light had appeared, a halo in the fog. There were voices.

"I tell you I heard something. Down there."

"Can you see anything?"

"No. Fetch the light this way. We ran into something."

"Where?"

Silas drummed with his heels.

"Listen!"

"Look, there's something down there!"

"Run to the afterdeck – quick! Throw the ladder over!"

There was a pounding of feet. The throb of the engine was very loud. The black cliff scraped past. Suddenly, with a rattle and splash, something tumbled into the water. Another light appeared, this time lower.

"Mr Mate! Look! There!"

"Quick, lad. Down you go."

"Give me a line! Give me a line!"

Again Silas drummed with his heels and made noises behind the gag. "Uuuhhh! Nnnnnn!"

Hand over hand, fast as a monkey, a sailor swarmed down the ladder as the *Sea Urchin* drifted past. He saw the huddled boy and made a grab for the boat's side but it was just out of reach. And the next moment Silas was drifting away, vanishing into the mist.

"I'm going in, boys!" the sailor shouted. "Hold fast!" With a spring and a splash he flung himself into the sea.

Four or five strokes brought him to the side of the little boat. With a gush of water and streaming head he hauled himself aboard. A light rope was between his teeth. Quickly he took a turn round one of the seats and bent to the boy who sprawled in a welter of fish. To his amazement the boy was bound and gagged.

The sailors were kind. They took Silas to the fo'c'sle, their big cabin in the bows of the ship, and wrapped him in a warm blanket while his clothes dried in the engine-room. Everyone saw, but nobody mentioned, the dirty tide-mark that ringed his neck. A mug of cocoa laced with rum steamed in his hands.

Fog and darkness pressed against the portholes.

"What about the *Sea Urchin*?" Silas asked anxiously.

"Don't worry, lad. Your boat's bobbing along behind."

The sailor who had rescued him sat at his side. He had changed into dry clothes. His blue eyes regarded Silas from beneath a fringe of wet hair.

"Now," he said. "Tell us what happened."

The fog did not lift. For a night and a day and a night the steamship *Morning Star*, homeward bound with a cargo of fruit from Pernambuco and Cadiz, swung at anchor a mile outside the breakwaters. Silas was worried about his grandfather and frightened for Ooli, but for the moment nothing could be done. He was given a hammock among the friendly sailors, and throughout the day helped them with their work on deck. In the evening he sat near the stove in the fo'c'sle and listened to their yarns, while every minute the fog bell rang overhead. Several had seen him around the harbour. He told them about his father and grandfather and his life as a rag-and-bone boy – but he did not tell them about the mermaid.

The sailor who had rescued him, broad and fresh-faced with a shock of fair hair, was called Dick Chatham. He wore a blue jersey and white trousers stained with oil and tar.

"And who was it," said Dick, "who tied you up like that and pushed you out in the fog?"

"Jasper Dredge," Silas said.

"Jasper Dredge!" exclaimed an older sailor. "He's a

bad lot that. Him *and* his son. How do you know Jasper Dredge?"

"Why'd he push you out to sea like that?" said another.

"Why didn't he take your boat?"

"And the fish?"

"How'd you catch so many?"

Silas looked to Dick for help.

"Stop quizzing the boy," Dick said. "He's telling the truth."

Silas nodded.

"But there's something else, isn't there."

He lowered his eyes.

"Well, we've all got secrets. You'll have your reasons. But remember," Dick clapped his bony back, "if ever you're in trouble you can call on the boys here. We're all your shipmates on the *Morning Star*."

"That's right." A sailor looked up from patching his britches. "You're a good 'un, young Silas Fisher. The way you helped out this morning and went up the rigging. You're all right."

The fo'c'sle door burst open, admitting a swirl of fog, and the ship's boy entered. He was only a year, possibly two, older than Silas. His name was Billy. In his hands was a tray piled high with Silas's fish, baked golden-brown, and wedges of hot bread.

A whiskery young seaman produced a concertina.

"Come on, lads," called another. "What about a drop of grog?"

In a moment a party was in full swing. Loud voices and sea shanties rang from the portholes into the dreary fog that pressed about the ship on all sides.

The following morning, though the air remained as thick as ever, the captain could put off the entry to harbour no longer. His cargo of fruit had to be fresh. Another cargo was waiting to be picked up.

"Mr Mate!" he called. "Let's put that boy's dinghy to some use. Two men in it; get them to row ahead with a line."

The anchor was weighed. Silas stood in the bow with Dick Chatham and stared ahead into the fog. Shouts of direction drifted back from the *Sea Urchin* and Dick called them up to the bridge. Slow as a ghost the *Morning Star* slid behind, engine throbbing softly, scarcely a swirl at the stern from the great propeller.

After a long time the lighthouse at the end of the breakwater materialized ahead, and an hour later the big steamship was moored alongside the quay. Families gathered to welcome the sailors home. Children came running to greet their fathers.

Silas thanked the captain – a ragged figure beside the fine braided uniform – and said goodbye to his friend Dick Chatham. Leaving the *Sea Urchin* tied to the bow, he descended the gangway. Then, trying not to collide with anything in the fog, he set off running through the docks and up the steep street to the rag-and-bone yard, to let his grandfather know that he was safe.

Chapter Seven

Into the Alleys

The gates of the rag-and-bone yard stood wide. Two children were rooting among the scrap. Silas grabbed a length of wood and sent them scuttling for their lives. The fog swallowed them up.

"Granda!" he called, but no whiskery face appeared at the window and when Silas opened the door he found the living-room empty. The fire lay dead. He went through the hall and up the uncarpeted stairs to the bedrooms. The house was deserted. Where was his grandfather? Had he been taken ill? Was he out searching?

He ran into the street and knocked at nearby doors.

"Have you seen my Granda?" he said to Granny Porter.

The old woman removed her pipe. "Haven't seen Old Silas for ever so long." Ancient eyes shone with interest.

"Why, has there been an accident?"

Silas returned home. For an hour he tidied the living-room and lit a fire in the grate. He boiled the black kettle and found half a dry loaf in the bread tin.

Midday came and went. The fog pressed its blind face against the window.

At length he decided to go searching. Neither Silas nor his grandfather could read or write, but a friendly trader had once taught him how to draw his name. Using a scrap of charcoal from the fire he scratched

SILAS

on a scrap of paper and left it on the table. Then, thinking of Jasper Dredge and the Alleys, he took an old seaman's knife from a drawer, the blade worn concave by years of sharpening. Silas treasured the knife for it had belonged to his father. As a young sailor his father had carved a sea-horse in the handle. Silas threaded the sheath on to the rope that held up his trousers.

As he did so there was a noise of coughing in the yard. The door opened, admitting a swirl of fog.

"Oh, Silas, boy! ... You're back!"

Weakly his grandfather grasped the back of a chair. His face was white, he was exhausted. Silas took his arm and helped him to a seat by the fire. The old man stretched bony hands towards the flames.

"Where," he struggled for breath, "where have you been?"

"Never mind me," Silas said. "What about you? You're sick, Granda. Shall I go for a doctor?"

Old Silas shook his head. "Doctors cost money . . . I'll be all right now. . . It's the fog – I can't breathe." He sank back in the chair. "Where have you been? Where's the lass? I've been that worried!"

"Well, I'm back now." Silas poured a cup of boiling water and put a big spoonful of rum in it. While his grandfather drank he told him all that had happened.

"That Jasper Dredge again! Poor lass!"

The old man's eyes closed and for an hour he slept. Silas split logs and piled the fire high. Tired after all his experiences, he lay back in the broken armchair. The salty logs crackled and spat, occasional flames burned blue and green. The tall clock struck the three-quarter hour.

Silas regarded its familiar face. His thoughts wandered. In every way it was a grandfather clock. More than a century earlier it had been made by Old Silas's grandfather, a master watchmaker, and passed down from father to son. In time it would belong to Silas also. Its silvery chimes were among his earliest memories. For years they had comforted him as he lay upstairs in bed and imagined murderers in the dark, or sea-monsters crawling up the street from the harbour. He half smiled –

then his thoughts returned to the present. His grand-father was sick. Ooli was somewhere out there in the fog.

Sweep yawned, showing needle-sharp teeth, and sprang on to Silas's lap.

The clock chimed the hour – and the quarter.

"What'll he do with her?" Silas said when his grand-father wakened.

"A real live mermaid?" He examined Silas's face. "Are you sure you want to know?"

He nodded.

"Well, you know Jasper Dredge. He'll show her, I expect, like a freak in a sideshow. Or sell her to a circus. She'll be worth a fortune."

"He can't! Not put her in a cage!"

"You did ask. One thing's sure, he won't keep quiet about it. She's not our secret any longer. The more people who know, the more money he'll make."

"But it'll kill her! She said she'd die! It's the one thing she's frightened of."

"I know."

Silas made a face. "Where would he show her?"

"Wherever there's a crowd." Old Silas coughed. "He'll take her round. Maybe in the market – or the fairground."

Silas thought. "What about the inns?"

"Certainly. Free drinks and a collection – yes, the inns most of all."

"I think I'll go out and start asking," Silas said.

"And if you find her – what then?"

"I don't know." Silas set another log on the fire. "Dick Chatham on the *Morning Star* – I could tell him."

"That's right, anyone but Old Silas!" His grandfather spoke bitterly. "Nothing but a wreck, just a blooming washout! If you could have seen me in the old days! If I didn't have this bad chest!"

"I know, Granda. I know. Don't worry." Silas pulled on his jacket. "You get strong again and show everybody."

"Here." His grandfather crossed to a corner and from beneath a loose floorboard lifted out a small wooden box, strapped with brass. He opened it with a little key from his waistcoat pocket, took out a washleather bag and extracted a shilling. "You might need this."

"No," Silas said. "Put it away. You keep it."

"Nonsense, boy, take it while you've got the chance. There's plenty more put by for emergencies."

"How much?"

"Never you mind – plenty!" He hid the box away and replaced the floorboard. "You'll be careful now, won't you. No silly risks."

Silas kissed his grandfather on his stubbly cheek. "Yes, Granda, I'll be careful."

The fog struck cold against his face. As he crossed the yard, the window faded to a yellow glow. Around him the piles of junk stood like sculptures in a strange landscape.

The November fog that lay over the city like a smothering blanket had brought down all the soot and sulphurous fumes from the sky. As the factory chimneys belched forth, the smoke sank across the roofs and filtered through narrow streets. The air was thick and grey and yellow; the roads were blind and full of the noise of coughing. Invisible horses neighed, carriages rattled past unseen. Boots sounded on the pavements, passers-by loomed up with handkerchiefs pressed across nose and mouth to keep out the poisonous air. Torches flared with yellow flame. Ragged beggars huddled in doorways.

Every street in the city had a pub or an inn, sometimes several. There were hundreds. Silas decided to start near the harbour, for sailors were free with their money and would readily pay to see a mermaid. Nervously he stopped outside the *Jolly Jack Tar* – then pushed open the door.

On that dreary afternoon the inn was a cavern of lamplight and warmth. Heady smells rose about him – beer and rum, sawdust and lamp oil. Men leaned on the bar and crowded about tables drawn near a glowing log fire. The arrival of a boy caused little interest, though some stared at his burst jacket and ragged trousers.

"Yes, my love," said a painted barmaid. "What can I get you?"

"I don't want a drink." Silas lowered his voice. "I'm looking for somebody."

"Looking for somebody!" She chucked him under the chin. "Who is it you're looking for, love?"

"Jasper Dredge," Silas whispered.

"Jasper Dredge!" she cried aloud. "We don't want the likes of him in here. What does a boy like you want with him?"

"He's —" Silas glanced sideways. "He's got a mermaid."

"What was that, love?" The barmaid leaned close. Silas was engulfed in a cloud of perfume.

"He's got a mermaid," he repeated shyly.

The barmaid regarded him with astonishment. "Get on, you saucy ha'porth!" Then seeing the expression on Silas's face she threw back her head and shrieked with laughter. "That's the best one yet. You hear that, boys?"

A score of sailors looked up from their drinks.

"This lad here's looking for Jasper Dredge. Says he's got a *mermaid*!"

A shout of laughter filled the room.

Silas stood his ground. "He has!" he cried courageously.

The laughter was redoubled. It was too much. Silas fled, his cheeks on fire.

For a quarter of a mile he ran headlong. The gas-lamps had been left burning all day, but no cheering necklace of lights spread down the road: one was reduced to a glow at his back before the next swam into sight. Silas stopped beneath a lamp-post. The mocking laughter still rang in his head.

But it must not stop his search. He peered around and caught the arm of a passing workman. The man pointed and went on his way. In three paces he had vanished into the gloom.

Silas headed for the city. He called at tavern after tavern – the *Monkey and Hornpipe*, the *Jigging Judge*, the *Ox and Chariot*, the *Foaming Dragon* and many others – but no one had seen Jasper Dredge in the past few days or knew anything of a mermaid.

A score of times he was lost. Peering over a wall at what he expected to be a railway line, Silas discovered the lapping water of the river. Turning into what he thought was the city market, he found himself among gravestones. And when he approached a group of stall-holders they drove him away angrily: "A mermaid! You're mad! Go on, get out of it!" Stones and rotten vegetables pursued him down the road.

Others were more helpful.

"Jasper Dredge and his like don't come into decent houses like this," the landlady of the *Whistling Gypsy* told him. "More likely you'll find him somewhere in the

Alleys. You want to try the *Murderer's Arms* or the *Fang and Gibbet*. But I wouldn't go near them places by yourself, dear – especially in weather like this. There's people just disappear. There's talk of pies, *meat* pies, that don't taste like pork or mutton – if you get my meaning."

"I've got to!" Silas was white. "It's special, see."

"Well, watch how you go. Only bit of advice I can give you – get hold of a club before you go in; nobody'll notice it in them streets. An eye in the back of your head and quick off the mark, that's the game. Keep your wits about you."

And so, greatly frightened and clutching a stout stick, Silas made his way from the fine squares into the dark, forbidden district of the city, the notorious Alleys. Fog-filled entrances and crooked passageways lay about him, all silent, a warren of whispers. Every corner and cob-webbed window seemed full of eyes. A distant cry made the air shiver. Taking a deep breath, Silas walked on.

In Wolf Lane, a street so narrow that the twisted buildings almost met overhead, he came upon a tavern. It was called the *Poisoned Cutlass*.

"And who is it who wants to know?" A tall and exceedingly thin man with hanging grey hair and broken teeth screwed the neck of Silas's jacket. "Who's asking for Jasper Dredge?"

His companion, a young albino, white-haired and

pink-eyed, picked his teeth with a dagger and looked on with interest. Two or three other figures, equally strange and alarming, sat at the bar and nearby tables.

"Who, eh? Who?"

"Just me." Silas wriggled helplessly.

"And what do you want him for?"

"Eli!" An enormously fat woman called from the end of the room. "Fetch 'im 'ere."

The tall man, stooped as a hairpin, gripped Silas's throat tighter and did not answer.

"Eli Clutch!" the woman said loudly. "I know what you're doin'! Leave 'is neck alone and bring 'im 'ere!"

The young albino stood aside. Reluctantly the other led Silas forward.

Though a fire burned at her side, the woman wore a long fur coat, as ragged and moth-eaten as the velvet settee on which she sat. Though she was old, untidy ringlets hung on her shoulders. Her eyes, Silas saw with a shiver, were as grey and blank as the fog outside.

"Right, Eli, push off!" She turned to Silas. "Now, young mister, sit down 'ere beside me. Give us your 'and."

Silas did as he was told. The woman took it in her lap. With tiny fingers, so fat they might have been inflated, and pinched by a dozen large rings – diamonds and rubies and emeralds that clicked like dice – she stroked the back of his hand and squeezed the knuckles of his fingers.

"That's nice," she said. "Just to get to know you, like. Not afraid o' Blind Nancy, are you?"

"No," Silas lied.

"Take no notice o' my Eli," she said. "Got no manners, 'e ain't. Now – " The fingers went on stroking and squeezing. "Who is it wants to see Jasper Dredge?"

"Me," Silas said.

With the speed of a snake the little hands wrenched back a finger. Silas shouted aloud.

"The truth, now!"

"I do!" Silas said. "Honest!"

"Well." The pressure was released, the fingers resumed their awful stroking. "And what do you want with Jasper Dredge?"

Silas hesitated.

"Remember, I can tell when you're lying," said Blind Nancy. "I can feel it."

"He's got a mermaid," Silas said.

"Ahhh!" The fingers massaged his knuckle as if to make it better. "Yes, I've 'eard of it. And what's that to you?"

"She's a friend of mine."

"And you wants to 'elp 'er escape, is that it?"

"No," Silas said, and cried out again as his finger was tugged halfway back to the wrist. "Yes! Yes!"

"That's better. And now I s'pose you expect me to give 'im warning."

"I don't know," Silas said.

"Well, let me tell you this. I 'ate Jasper Dredge!" Letting go of Silas's hand, she hooked back the collar of her coat. A livid scar ran down her neck and one shoulder. "It was 'im done this to me. Tried to spoil my pretty good looks. Drunk, 'e was, like an animal. Would've murdered me if he'd got 'alf a chance!" She smiled coquettishly and drew fingers through her straggling grey ringlets. "So if you can get that mermaid away from 'im, then Nancy'll be pleased. Got great plans for 'er, 'im an' that disgustin' son of 'is."

"Do you know where he's keeping her?" said Silas.

"Course I do. There's nothing Blind Nancy doesn't know. But afore I tell you – what present 'ave you got for me? I like presents. See my rings." She held out one hand. The chipped jewels flashed like fire in the lamplight. "They was all presents. Pretty, aren't they?"

"Yes," Silas said.

"Presents from my 'usband when we was first married. Wasn't they, Eli?" She turned her head. "A good-lookin' man 'e was then, taking ways, though you wouldn't think it to look at 'im now. 'Asn't kept 'is looks like me. 'Eard of Strangler Clutch, 'ave you?"

"No," Silas said.

"Afore your time, I expect. Gone down in the world.

Ah, well! Now – " She resumed stroking Silas's hand. "What about that present?"

"I haven't got anything," said Silas.

"What, nothing?" The fat hands faltered and squeezed a knuckle.

"Well, there's this knife." Silas took it from the sheath at his waist. "It belonged to my father."

"Don't want no knives. Got enough knives, 'aven't we, Pinky?"

"Always do with another." The albino had a high voice. A tear spilled from one red-rimmed eye. "Makes a change."

"No, it's not up to your standard, Pinky." The jewelled fingers ran over the worn blade and wooden handle. "Just a cheap job – rusty an' all. Let 'im keep it. 'Sides, he might need it if he's goin' after Jasper Dredge." She thrust it back at Silas. "What else've you got? Any money?"

"I've got a shilling," Silas said reluctantly.

"A shillin'! Let's 'ave it – quick!"

Silas fumbled in his pocket and produced the coin. In a flash the fat fingers tweaked it away and hid it inside the fur coat.

"What else?"

"Nothing," said Silas.

"I don't believe you." Impatiently Blind Nancy began rummaging through his clothes. The little hands thrust into his pockets and inside his jacket, even beneath his ragged jersey, lest he wore a chain or locket at his throat. "Nothin'!" she spat. "Nothin' at all! What are you, a beggar?"

"A rag-and-bone boy," said Silas.

"A rag-and-bone – ! An' 'ere you are sittin' beside me on my lovely velvet settee!" She pushed him away violently and wiped her fingers on a filthy lace handkerchief. "Go on, get out of it! What d'you think you're doin', Eli, lettin' scum like that into my nice clean parlour?"

Nervously Silas stood his ground. "Where will I find Jasper Dredge?" he said.

"Never you mind that! Get out o' my 'ouse!"

"You promised!" Silas said. "I give you a shilling!"

"I promised! Why, you – " She paused then gave a bark of laughter. "You've got guts, I'll give you that. You've got nerve. You want Jasper Dredge – well, you'll find 'im at the *Black Parrot* in 'Angman Square. That's 'is usual 'angout: 'e's the landlord. An' now, if you're not out of 'ere afore I count to five, I'll let Eli and Pinky loose at you. One – two – three – "

Dodging blows and legs that were thrust out to trip him up, Silas fled from the tavern. At once the fog closed about him. As he ran up Wolf Lane, a guffaw of harsh laughter sounded at his back.

There was another noise too. He stopped and listened. The soft pad of footsteps. Somebody was following.

There was a murmur of voices. He sprinted and dodged aside into a black doorway. The footsteps drew closer. Eli Clutch and Pinky appeared momentarily in the glow of a gas lamp.

"Such a nice young neck!" Eli panted. "So smooth!"

"An' a rusty knife!" came Pinky's high-pitched tones. "Oh my! When we get hold of him, Eli!"

"What pies 'e'll make!"

Their footsteps faded into the fog. At once Silas slipped from his hiding place and ran back the way he had come. He passed the windows of the *Poisoned Cutlass*, and five minutes later the fearful tavern and the two murderers were far behind him.

Chapter Eight

The *Black Parrot*

O f all notorious inns – from the *Dead o' Night* in Cornwall to the *Rotting Skull* in Yorkshire and the *Adder's Nest* near Inverness – the *Black Parrot* had the most fearsome reputation. Robbers and highwaymen gathered there, pickpockets, murderers, criminals of every description. It was the hub of all that was wicked in the teeming city. Any ruffian who was on the run from the law made his way to the *Black Parrot*, for there lay safety.

It stood at the heart of the Alleys, amid the ruins of Hangman Square. Crooked houses rose on all sides, weeds sprouted between the paving stones. Like a broken wing, the spire of a deserted church hung against the sky. The few trees that survived had been mutilated for firewood. Scavengers, the hollow-cheeked scum of the city, had made dens in the cellars and fallen masonry.

Stray cats slid through the passageways hunting for rats. Even in midsummer the place had a sinister air. After the sun had set, no honest man dared enter the once-prosperous square. Only villains slipped along the pavements, dodging from shadow to shadow. Every so often the darkness was punctuated by a scream or drunken shout.

For an hour Silas felt his way through the foggy lanes, terrified of bumping into Pinky and Eli, frightened to ask the way, for he had left his cudgel at the *Poisoned Cutlass*. Night had long fallen as he crept through the ruins of Hangman Square, and the grim silhouette of the *Black Parrot* rose before him.

It was a dark, lopsided building of beams and dirty plaster. Each of the upper storeys overhung the one below and the crooked roof was topped by tall chimneys, now shrouded in darkness. The studded door stood ajar, exhaling a breath of rum and drunken voices. Dim yellow rays from the bull's-eye windows touched the hanging sign, a wicked black parrot with a claw full of gold. Sinister figures gathered against the wall in the gloom.

Silas paused on the pavement.

"What are you starin' at?" snarled a gaunt man in black with a ragged scar down one cheek.

"I wasn't staring," Silas said.

"Don't bandy words wi' me, you young dog!"

The man stepped forward and raised a heavy stick. Silas backed into the street. His heel skidded on something soft – a dead rat? rotting fruit? – and he fell sidelong into a broad gutter that ran through the cobbles. A crippled beggar laughed shrilly. The heavy stick struck his begging-bowl and scattered the few coins that lay within. One tinkled past Silas and dropped through a large iron grille. Briefly it fell and plopped into the open drain beneath.

"'Ere, Carver, there was no need for that!" The beggar's voice was a whine. Dodging a second blow, he snatched up his coins and scuttled away into the night.

Silas retreated and approached the inn from another direction. A cobbled yard opened before him, dimly lit by a lantern at the back door of the inn. The earth was strewn with straw and trampled dung; two or three horses champed in black stalls. Abruptly he came upon his cart, abandoned against a stone wall. His heart thudded. He stared about in the fog.

Poised for flight, Silas circled the outbuildings. Some contained casks, logs, broken harness. Others were locked. He knocked softly. "Ooli! Ooli! Are you there? It's me, Silas."

There was no reply.

The door opened at the rear of the inn and a man emerged, silhouetted against the lantern light. Silas ducked into the shadows. The man crossed the yard. A horse whinnied softly, horseshoes clattered on the cobbles. The man rode off.

Silas stared after him then crossed to the black inn door. For a minute he listened intently, then inched the door open. The voices came clearly now. A gas-lit corridor lay before him. Crooked doorways opened on either side, a flight of steps led down to the cellar. At the end of the corridor a glow of light proclaimed the bar-room. A sudden outburst of noise – the shouts of men and laughter of loud women – made him duck back into the yard.

If Blind Nancy had spoken the truth and Jasper Dredge had not sold her, then Ooli was imprisoned in the *Black Parrot* itself. In one of the upper rooms? In the cellar? Silas trembled. He pushed the door wide, ready for escape, and advanced into the corridor. The gas-jets hissed softly. There was a smell of sweat, tobacco and rum.

On either side lay kitchens and storerooms. They were deserted. Cleavers lay on greasy tables; geese and salted pigs hung from hooks; crates of contraband tea, casks of butter, barrels of stolen oranges, stood against the walls. On tiptoe Silas moved forward. The flight of stone steps which led to the cellar was close to the bar-room door. He peered down into the gloom and began to descend. Though he trod carefully, his boots made a noise. He tugged them off. As he did so there was a sound of footsteps. Barefoot he fled down the stairs and pressed back into the shadows.

"Someone's left this door open." He recognized the voice. It was Albert Dredge. "Be havin' thieves in next. Want to be more careful." With a bang the door was shut, a bolt rattled.

The footsteps receded.

Silas emerged from his hiding place. He stood in a flagged and winding passage. The smell of beer was strong. So was the stink of mould and damp. Water oozed from stone walls and trickled to the floor, cold beneath his feet. More storerooms lay on either side. Casks and crates smelled of brandy and new tobacco. He pushed open a studded door and saw an outline of barrels. It was the beer cellar.

Further down the passage, at the foot of three steps, was a similar door. Heavy manacles and a length of rope hung from a peg outside. The door was locked. Silas stared over his shoulder and knocked softly.

"Ooli!" he breathed. "Are you there? It's me, Silas."

The door was strapped with iron. From beyond came a soft bump and a slither, then a voice.

"Oh, Silas!" There was a sound of weeping.

"Have they hurt you? Are you all right?"

"No, they have not hurt me but – Oh, Silas, you must get me out! If you don't I shall die!"

There was a noise of scratching at the door and a soft whine.

"What's that?" Silas said.

"The big man's dog. He's locked in here with me."

"That savage yellow brute! Be careful it doesn't bite you."

"He isn't savage. The big man starves him and beats him. He's frightened. Shhh, Bosun! There!" Softly she spoke and the dog was quiet.

"Have you been locked down here all the time?"

"No. They – " the mermaid could not control her weeping – "they show me in yards and in the town. Two nights, two whole days! They'll be coming again soon. Get me out, Silas!"

"The door's locked. I have no key. But now I know where you are – "

There was a sudden sound of voices approaching. Heavy footsteps started down the cellar stairs. Lantern light flashed on the walls. Silas stared back along the passage then darted to the door of the beer cellar. All was black. Barefoot he felt his way across the vault and ducked behind a row of enormous barrels. A moment later the door swung wide and Jasper Dredge entered. His sleeves were rolled high, a barman's apron was around his middle. Gnawing the remains of half a roast hen, Albert followed at his father's heels.

"I didn't leave this door open," said Jasper.

"Me neither." Albert munched. "The back door was open an' all."

"Someone been snoopin' round, do you think?" Jasper seized a wooden mallet and knocked the bung from a new cask of beer. "No, they wouldn't dare. They know what happened to the last one." Briskly he tapped in the pipes from the bar overhead and bowled the empty cask to the end of the row.

"Time to take *her* up now, Pa?" Albert said eagerly.

"Must be about." Jasper felt in his waistcoat pocket and held a large gold watch to the lantern. "All right, if you like." He rumpled his son's hair. "You enjoy that, don't you?"

"I like collectin' the money," Albert said. "An' the way she lashes out an' hisses an' everythin'." He sniggered at the memory. "One day, when you've got her tamed, I'm goin' to take her out fishin', the way she did with that Silas Fisher."

He sucked the last piece of meat from a bone and slung the straggling carcass of the hen into a corner. As he did so, Silas eased his bare foot from a stone. His toes nudged a boot. There was a tiny rattle.

"What was that?" Albert stared across.

"Only a rat," his father said. "Come in from the drains. Not surprisin', the way you sling old bones about the place."

They returned to the door. The lantern flung grotesque shadows on the wall.

"What do you think happened to 'im, Pa?"

"Who?"

"Silas Fisher, o' course."

"Down in Davy Jones's locker by now, I reckon. Or dead o' the cold. No one would pick 'im up in fog like this."

"That's rich! Good riddance to bad rubbish!" Albert sniggered again. "Eh, Pa?"

The door shut and the cellar was plunged into darkness.

Silas massaged his foot. The fumes from the beer kegs made him light-headed. Helplessly he listened as Ooli's door was unlocked, and pressed hands over his ears to muffle her cries and the Dredges' laughter as the iron manacles were snapped round her wrists and the rope was fastened from tail to neck. The dog barked loudly. There was an angry oath and a blow. With a yelp the dog fell silent. Then heavy footsteps retreated along the passage and mounted the stairs to the ground floor of the inn.

Cautiously, boots in hand, Silas emerged from the beer cellar. The mermaid's door stood open. He peered into the dirty chamber. There was no window. The ugly dog, still trembling, stood tied to a ring-bolt in the wall. Ooli had gone.

A shout overhead greeted her arrival in the bar-room.

Feet drummed on the floor, glasses thudded on the tables.

Fearful that the dog would start barking again, Silas hurried away. Silently he flitted up the cellar steps. Right and left he peeped along the corridor. The coast was clear. Seconds later he stood in the comparative safety of the inn yard.

His feet were cold and dirty. He scrubbed them with a handful of straw and pulled on his boots.

The fog pressed close. Distressed by all he had seen and heard, Silas wondered what he could do. Cautiously he explored the outside of the inn, peering through windows. Most were dark, and where light shone across the pavement of the square, Carver and his shadowy companions still kept their vigil. Two windows glowed yellow at the side of the inn. Silas pressed his face to the bull's-eye panes. It was the bar-room. Voices came loudly, colours and shapes moved within, but he could distinguish nothing through the distorting glass.

He returned to the inn yard.

Several minutes later the back door opened and a boy came out. A lantern hung from his hand. He crossed the murky yard and opened one of the outbuildings with a bunch of keys.

Silas peered through the entrance. It was the pot-boy of the inn, who served the drinkers with their ale and rum. He wore britches, unlaced below the knee, and a dirty green smock. A greasy cap was set jauntily on his head. Busily he stacked logs into a basket to carry them into the inn.

"Hey!" Silas stood in the doorway.

The pot-boy jumped. "Don't do that!" he said. "Not on a dark night, not round 'ere. End up wiv a knife in your guts."

Silas advanced into the lantern light. The boy regarded him suspiciously.

"What d'you want?" .

Silas nodded. "Is it right they've got a mermaid in there?"

"Yeah, they 'ave. Long 'air an' a silver tail." The pot-boy grinned. "Smashin' she is."

"I'd like to see her," Silas said.

"Well, why don't you? Go inside an' buy a drink, pay your sixpence."

"I haven't got sixpence."

"Well, you can't see 'er then. That's simple enough." With a grunt he swung his basket towards the entrance.

"What do they do with her?" Silas said.

'Well, they just – " He broke off. "You've got a lot o' questions."

Silas shrugged. "A mermaid – wouldn't you?"

"What's your name?"

"Jack," Silas said promptly. "Jack Holland."

"An' you really want to see the mermaid." The pot-boy scratched his head. "Well, there might be a way."

Silas leaned forward.

"I could lend you my smock for five minutes," the boy said. "We're more or less the same 'ight."

Silas hesitated. "My hair's different," he said. "I'm thinner. They'd know it wasn't you straight away."

"Nah! Not if we swapped trousers an' all, an' you put on the cap. They're all 'alf drunk in there anyway; no one would know the diff'rence. Even if they did, who cares, 's long as they get their rum."

As if to confirm his words, a drunken clamour rose on the night.

"If you're frightened, o' course!" The pot-boy pulled a cigar-butt from his pocket, examined it critically, and lit it at the lantern.

"Who's frightened?" Silas pretended a boldness he did not feel. "All right, then. Give us the smock."

"It'll cost you," said the pot-boy. "You see the mermaid for nothin'. What do I get out of it?"

Silas rummaged through his pockets and laid their contents on top of a box. The pot-boy poked through the pieces of string, coloured pebbles, candle-stubs, lucky hare's foot and other items of no value.

"That all you got?" he said contemptuously.

Silas flushed. "What about this?" He held out his tinder-box.

"I got one already – better than that." The boy rose. "Come on, I got to lock up."

Reluctantly Silas loosened the rope that held up his trousers and slid off his father's sea-knife in its leather sheath. "I've got this."

The knife was better than Blind Nancy had realized. There was only a trace of rust on the worn blade, the little sea-horse was beautifully carved. The pot-boy examined it and tested the edge with his thumb.

"I got a knife an' all." He hesitated. "Well, yes, all right. Five minutes, mind. No longer."

He set the knife out of Silas's reach and pulled the dirty smock over his head.

"That's for the knife. If you want the rest I'll take – " He picked out the best of the items Silas had taken from his pockets, then pulled off his cap.

In a minute they had exchanged clothes. Silas felt strange pulling on the still-warm shirt and britches. He was frightened. His stomach quaked as he heaved the basket of logs to his back.

"You'll be here when I get back?" he said.

The pot-boy nodded, whittling a scrap of wood with Silas's treasured knife.

"You'll not play any tricks?" Silas pulled the cap to his eyebrows. "No double-crossing."

"Why should I? Jus' drop the logs at the side o' the fire, stir it up a bit, then go through where you 'ear the shoutin'." Dagger-like he threw the knife into an empty keg and puffed on his cigar-butt.

Bowed beneath his load of logs, Silas took up the lantern and crossed the foggy yard. The black door loomed before him. He mounted the worn step and made his way along the corridor towards the shouts and thudding glasses of the bar-room.

Dark beams ran overhead, gas-lamps threw a yellow glow upon a tumultuous scene. Villainous-looking men – bearded ruffians and mad-eyed desperadoes, cloaked highwaymen and soil-stained body-snatchers, crop-headed convicts and wreckers in sea-boots – sprawled in chairs and hugged their lady-friends. Their jackets were loosened, weapons hung at their hips. Bottles of rum and tankards of ale stood on every table, chains of foam spilled to the sawdust-scattered floor. The air was ripe with the smell of sweat and perfume and spirits. Every-one was shouting. After the silence of the fog, the noise was tremendous.

"About time, too!" a fat barman roared at Silas. "Come on, you lazy good-for-nothing! Stoke up the fire! There's men want rum here – rum and ale and brandy-wine!"

As Silas staggered towards the hearth a heavy hand slapped him on the seat of his britches, a thigh-boot was thrust out to trip him up. At the same moment a roar erupted in a room beyond the bar. Silas looked across, eyes shadowed by his cap.

Albert Dredge stood in the doorway, laughing at whatever was taking place within. His shirt-sleeves were rolled up, he wore a waistcoat and red neckerchief. One hand jingled a heavy bag of coins at his waist.

Silas had often been in bars, he had seen pot-boys at work. Briskly he stacked the logs by the fire, set a couple on the embers and crossed to the counter.

"Flagon o' rum!" he said gruffly.

The fat barman slapped it down and Silas carried it away. As he reached the doorway of the inner room, Albert Dredge stood aside to let him past. A moment later the new pot-boy was lost among the shoulders and clashing sword-hilts of the throng. A raucous cheer rose on all sides. He pushed forward – and all at once there was Ooli, right before him.

To make a better show they had removed the manacles and neck rope. Now her wrists were tied to the arms of a wooden chair which they had set on a table so that all could see. Rough hands thrust forward to squeeze her silver tail. Jasper Dredge pulled back her head and tipped a foaming tankard to her lips.

He looked like a demon, red-bearded, his mouth hot and wide, tufts of hair sprouting from ear and nostril.

Ooli twisted her head aside, lips pressed tight. The ale spilled down her arm. Though they had rubbed her with an old cloth, her hair was matted, her bright tail streaked with dirt from the floor of the cellar. Several stale herring, which Jasper had tried to force her to eat, lay scattered on the table. In desperation she cried aloud and lashed out with her tail. Women screamed. Those nearest the table sprang back, slopping rum down their jackets, and shouted with laughter.

Silas could not bear it. Tears of outrage pricked his eyes. But only for a moment. A hand tapped him on the shoulder. He turned and found himself staring into the face of Albert Dredge. At his side the pot-boy, ragged in Silas's clothes, grinned with malicious pleasure.

"I was right, wasn't I, Albert?" the pot-boy said. "I remembered what you told me. It *is* 'im, isn't it."

"Yeah, it's 'im, all right. You did good, Sammy. I'm pleased with yer."

Silas darted back, but his way was blocked by the press of bodies round the table. Albert seized him by the smock. Silas flung the flagon of rum into his face. There was a loud cry and a brief, fierce battle. The table lurched. Ooli's chair toppled among the crowd of outlaws and villains. The ropes binding her arms fell loose. Her eyes were wild. With lacerating nails she lashed out at her tormentors. Her silver tail knocked them from their feet.

It was a brave fight but it could not succeed. Her arms were seized, her wrists retied, and a minute later she was a prisoner again.

The excited crowd drew back around two figures on the floor. Silas lay spreadeagled with Albert Dredge sitting upon his chest. Helplessly he bucked and struggled. Albert's thick lips parted in a smile.

"Well, if it ain't my old friend Silas Fisher – or should I call you Jack? Back from a watery grave, large as life. How *very* nice to see you again!"

Chapter Nine

The Dripping Prison

The pressing crowd laughed as Silas was made to strip off the pot-boy's smock and britches and pull on his own ragged clothes.

"Where d'you get the shiv, Sammy?" Albert Dredge pulled the sea-knife from its sheath and turned it admiringly.

"He give it me, for the change of clothes." The pot-boy grinned. "Good trick, eh?"

"Yeah, smart!" Albert loosened his buckle and slid the knife on to his belt. "I'll 'ave that."

"Ah, but that's mine! Come on, give it back!" The pot-boy made a snatch.

Albert cuffed him lightly on the ear. "You never remember, do you, Sammy. What's yours is mine and what's mine's my own. 'Sides, you got this by a dirty trick on my pal Silas, 'ere. Silas an' me's got an understandin'." He brandished the knife before Silas's face. "Yeah, he does what I tell 'im, or I cut 'is ears off!"

"You wait!" Silas struggled in the grip of a man in a shabby frock coat who smelled of brandy. "I'll get even with you! You're a bully! A coward!" He struck out with sharp knuckles. "You're yellow right through, Albert Dredge!"

"Why, you cheeky – " The fat youth thrust the knife back into its sheath and clenched a fist. "I'll flatten your face for you!"

"All right, Albert. That's enough!" Jasper Dredge spoke roughly. "Take 'im downstairs and fling 'im in the cellar. We'll decide what to do with *'im* later. We're in the middle of a show, 'ere. Men've paid money."

Scowling, Albert grasped Silas by the collar and dragged him away. The crowd pressed aside to let them through. Fighting all the way, Silas looked back and saw Ooli in Jasper's grasp. Her eyes were desperate.

"Silas!" she cried. "Silas!"

Then the crowd intervened and she was hidden from sight. Still struggling, Silas was hauled and kicked through the main bar-room into the corridor, down the twisting cellar steps, and along the passage to Ooli's prison.

"Right!" With a final shove, Albert sent him sprawling into the dirt of the cellar floor. "You can cool your 'eels in there for a day or two – till Pa an' me decides what to do with you." He leered into the shadows. "I promise you one thing – it'll be 'orrible. Whatever you *think* we might do, it's goin' to be worse – a hundred times worse. An' remember, like I told the mermaid, shout as much as you like, there's no one to 'ear you, no one who cares. But get on my nerves an' I'll come down 'ere an' cut your tongue out! All right?"

Fouled with mud, Silas looked up at the figure silhouetted in the entrance. Then the door slammed shut and he was plunged into darkness. Keys rattled at the lock, heavy footsteps receded along the passage.

Silas pulled himself to his hands and knees. He waited for his eyes to accustom themselves to the darkness, but no chink of light appeared beneath the door or from a boarded-up window. A rumble of feet and occasional shouts came from the bar-room overhead. Apart from this he might have been imprisoned in the blackness and silence of a grave.

Then a soft whine came from the mongrel tied near the door.

Silas felt in his pockets. His battered tinder-box was still there, so were the two or three candle-stubs. He rubbed his muddy fingers against his trousers and struck a spark into the dry tinder, blew it alive and touched a light to a wick. The candle burned up bravely and cast flickering shadows about the walls. Carefully Silas set it on a ledge and looked around his prison.

The cellar was quite large, eight or ten metres long and half as broad, with an arched stone roof. Fungus grew in the corners and seeping water formed puddles on the earth floor. A scatter of empty kegs and mouldy sacks lay at the inner end. Apart from these it was bare.

With one of the cleaner sacks Silas scrubbed the mud from his face and clothes, then crossed to examine the door. As he came close the dog strained on its rope, cowering and whining in a desperate effort to please. Silas regarded the big bulldog head, the wrinkled face and torn ear, and remembered how it had lunged and snarled when Jasper Dredge had it on a leash. Cautiously he put out a hand but as Ooli had said, there was nothing to fear now.

"There, Bosun," he said softly. "Who's a good boy."

As he crouched to pat it, the dog sprang up to lick his face, shivering and yelping with pleasure.

The door was solid. He twisted the handle and pushed, but it was securely locked. There was no possibility of breaking it open, a door like that could have withstood a battering ram, let alone a skinny boy.

The candle stubs would not last long. Silas untied the dog and retreated to the end of the cellar. Some of the barrels were rotted with age but one or two were sound. He toppled a hogshead on to its side and bowled it to the driest part of the floor. He rolled another beside it for Ooli, laid sacks in each, and spread another on the earth for Bosun to lie on. Then, for the cellar was cold, he stepped right inside one of the sacks, tugged it about his shoulders, and retreated into the overturned barrel. He had lifted the candle from its ledge and now blew it out. Stretching out a thin hand in the darkness, he touched Bosun's paw and nose. With a warm tongue the mongrel licked his fingers.

For a long time Silas lay thinking: wondering what was happening to Ooli; terrified what Jasper Dredge and Albert might do to him. Words came back: "Get in my way again an' I'll 'ave your liver for breakfast... Snoopin' round – they wouldn't dare, they know what 'appened to the last one... I'll come down 'ere an' cut your tongue out... Tie a stone round 'is neck an' drop 'im overboard!" He pictured his grandfather, coughing and frail, peering into the fog from the gates of the scrapyard. He thought of Ooli swimming and laughing – Ooli from the Islands of the Sun: "... ridden whales in the jade-green seas of the equator ... chased penguins beneath the floating ice-mountains of the south." And now – tied up and dirty, shown off to ruffians in a barroom. What had she said? "Some mermaids never return – I may not myself."

Silas felt his chest tighten. A tear slid down his nose. The dog whined and crept closer.

At length, exhausted by the events of a long day – a day that had led him from the fog-bound *Morning Star* to the rag-and-bone yard, the inns of the city, Blind Nancy, the *Black Parrot*, and finally into imprisonment – he sank into a troubled sleep.

He was wakened, there was no way of knowing how long afterwards, by a rattle at the door and the sound of voices. Staring up, eyes pricking with sleep, Silas saw a dazzle of lantern-light and black figures.

"Right, in you go!" A burly man – it was Jasper Dredge – descended the cellar steps. The mermaid was in his arms. As if she were a sack of rubbish, he dumped her on the muddy floor. "You can get your scruffy pal to untie your 'ands an' tail. Albert," he stepped aside, "'ave you got the bread an' water?"

A jug and broken loaf were set by the wall.

"Oh, there y'are." Albert saw Silas blinking from the barrel. "Havin' nice dreams, were you? Thinkin' about what me an' Pa's goin' to do?" He laughed.

Father and son retreated up the steps.

"Right, then, we'll be down tomorrow!" Jasper's voice was thick with rum. "Show you off to a few more o' my pals. The money's comin' in very nicely." He had taken the bag from Albert and shook it heavily. "A proper gold mine, you are. Goo'night! Sleep well!"

The door banged, the lock snapped shut. As the footsteps receded, Silas realized that all sound had ceased from the bar-room overhead. It was very late.

But the hour did not matter. Heart-breaking sobs

came from the mermaid hidden in the darkness.

"I'm here." Silas fumbled for his tinder-box. "Don't cry."

He set the flickering candle-stub on his overturned barrel and crossed to Ooli. Her shoulders shook. As well as he was able he helped her across the cellar and wiped away the worst of the mud. Luckily there was plenty of water. He and Ooli drank from the jug and Bosun lapped from his hand, then he poured some over the mermaid's hair to rinse out the dirt, and more down her silver tail. Side by side they lay down in the two barrels and Silas blew out the candle.

"Oh, it was awful, horrible!" Ooli could not check her sobs. "They took me to inn yards and greasy taverns. The boy collected money. They locked me in cages and tried to make me swim in horse-troughs. Drunkards came staring and poking with their dirty hands. A woman wanted to cut off my hair to make a wig. Another said if I died the big man should take me to a taxidermist! He said it was a good idea! ... Oh, Silas, I can fight sharks and octopuses and savage eels, but not that! And what that boy says they're going to do to you –! It's all my fault!"

"Nonsense!" Silas said stoutly. "And you're not going to die – we're going to escape. All three of us. I don't know how, but we are." He broke off a chunk of bread and passed it across. "Now come on, eat something. You've got to keep up your strength, you'll need it."

He tore off another piece of bread for Bosun and a good crust for himself.

For a long time they lay talking. Little by little the mermaid's distress quietened.

Outside a breeze whispered from the north. The fog that for days had lain like a blanket over the city began to stir. Wreaths drifted round the gas-lamps and coiled about the roofs and forest of chimneys. Fingers of chill, clean air felt along the city streets. The breeze became a sea wind. In an hour it was possible to see a hundred metres. In two, a watcher on a church tower could see lights twinkling on the far side of the city. The fog had gone.

But in the cellar beneath the *Black Parrot* all was still. No breeze, no chink of starlight, no pink glow of dawn entered that dripping chamber. Three heads together, the boy, the mermaid and the yellow dog slept deeply in the silence of their prison.

Chapter Ten

Shipmates

F ar from the *Black Parrot*, in the rag-and-bone yard above the harbour, Old Silas waited. Reckless with fuel he stacked the fire high to drive out the fog and have a warm welcome for his grandson when he returned. But Silas did not return. Hour by hour the November day crawled past – and then the night. The fog dispersed. The stars faded. A clear dawn shone through the yard window.

At nine o'clock, frail and coughing, he made his way through the streets to the office of the city constabulary.

"My grandson," said Old Silas. "He went out yesterday afternoon in the fog and didn't come back. Something's happened to him."

But in those days the city was full of waifs – homeless children who lived by their wits and slept in doorways, in forgotten attics among the high chimneys, beneath carts in the market place. No one was interested in a ragboy who had wandered off and failed to return.

Hoping forlornly that Silas might have turned up in his absence, the old man clutched his collar against the wind and trailed homeward.

At midday his heart leaped at the sound of footsteps and a lively rat-tat-tat on the yard door. He hurried to pull it open. Two sailors stood at the entrance, Dick Chatham and a curly-headed shipmate. It was Saturday; their morning's work finished, they were free for the weekend. The sun shone at their backs, coloured neck-erchiefs and bell-bottomed trousers flapped in the wind.

"Mr Fisher?" Dick held out a hand. "We're off the *Morning Star*. Young Silas probably told you about us. Is he in?"

"I'm afraid not." Old Silas's hand, once so strong, was a bundle of bones in the friendly grasp. "I don't know where he is, boys. He went out yesterday to look for a friend – and he hasn't come back." He hesitated. "I don't think he told you about the mermaid."

"The mermaid?" The sailors shook their heads.

"Look, come in by the fire, lads." Old Silas stood aside. "It's a poor place but you're welcome."

Dick carried a set of clothes and oilskins, too small now for his brother but just right for Silas. The second sailor, a gypsy-looking fellow named Peter, carried a cake, newly-baked by his wife. They set their gifts on the table and followed the old man to the fireside.

"A grand lad, young Silas."

"Helped us on deck."

"A real first-rater." Dick perched on the edge of the settee. "We're having a bit of a party on board tonight – families and sweethearts and friends. We hoped you'd both come down and join us."

"I wish we could, boys." Old Silas wiped his eyes with a ragged handkerchief.

"Come on, Pop." Peter squeezed his shoulder. "Tell us what happened."

Wide-eyed they listened to the story of Silas and Ooli. It was soon told.

"What do you think?" Dick turned to his companion.

"We go and look for him, of course." Peter stood up. "Right now. That Jasper Dredge is a nasty piece of work."

Dick buttoned his jacket and followed him to the door. "Leave it to us, Mr Fisher. You keep the fire built up and try not to worry. I'll be surprised if we don't have word of him before the day's out."

And so, throughout that cold November afternoon, the two sailors hunted in the market and fairground, and through all the inns and taverns of the great city.

"That's right," said the laughing barmaid of the *Jolly Jack Tar*. "He was here, looking for Jasper Dredge. Something about a mermaid – daft young ha'porth."

"No, I haven't seen him," said the owner of the *Cock and Cannon*. "What are you drinking, boys?"

"I don't know where he went." The landlord of the *Jigging Judge* hiccuped tipsily. "He just vanished into the fog."

"Yes, he was here," said the landlady of the *Whistling Gypsy*. "A plucky lad, very determined. I told him to ask in the Alleys. He went alone. I told him it wasn't safe."

"Oh my!" Blind Nancy turned her fogged grey eyes upon the pair who entered the *Poisoned Cutlass*, clubs in their hands. "Fine young sailors, smelling of the sea. Come to see Blind Nancy." Girlishly she pinched her cheeks and tossed the grey ringlets. "'Ere, Crippen." She summoned the barman. "Fetch us a bottle o' brandy and glasses for my friends. So, you're looking for the rag-and-bone boy. Well, I know what *I* told 'im, but you'd better ask Eli and Pinky – they might know something we don't." A fat cat watched from her moth-eaten lap as she scratched it with jewelled fingers. "'Ave you brought me a present?"

And so it was, as shadows deepened in the Alleys on that Saturday afternoon, that Dick and his shipmate found themselves on the pavement outside the *Black Parrot*. Confronted by two armed seamen, the scavengers backed towards the ruins of Hangman Square and watched.

"Jasper Dredge!" Dick raised his voice. "Are you in

there? Come on out; there's somebody wants to see you!"

Villainous faces appeared at the windows of the *Black Parrot* – scarred cheeks, eye-patches, snarling mouths. A moment later Jasper appeared in the doorway. His red hair was wild, a rusty cutlass hung from one hand. Ruffians followed at his back, more spilled out from the side door of the inn. The seamen were outnumbered, four to one. They backed to avoid being surrounded.

"Who are you?" Jasper raised a bottle to his lips. "What d'you want with Jasper Dredge?"

"We're looking for a boy – Silas Fisher by name." Dick stepped forward. "You took something that belonged to him. He come looking for you to get it back."

"So?"

"He's disappeared."

"What's that to do wi' me? What is it I'm supposed to have taken?"

Dick hesitated. "A mermaid," he said stoutly. "She was in his care."

"A mermaid!" The villains burst into raucous mirth. "Was she ridin' a sea-'orse?"

"Very funny!" Dick flushed. "You're a great joker, Jasper Dredge. But we're looking for the boy. Where is he?"

"Mermaids? Boys? I don't know what you're talkin' about. All that bouncin' about on the sea's loosened your brains. Now go on, get out of it, afore I set the mob on you!"

He raised his cutlass and advanced on the ruddy young seaman. Dick drew the cudgel from his belt.

"We know you've got the mermaid, you've been showing her about. Blind Nancy told us – and others. But right now it's the boy we're looking for. A skinny lad in a ragged jacket. You know who I mean – the one you set adrift. And I reckon he's here, or somewhere nearby."

Despite his strength and cutlass and followers, Jasper was a coward. He eyed the determined Dick and hid his fear behind an oath and black scowl.

"An' I'm telling you I 'aven't seen 'im!" He appealed to his ferocious companions. "Has he been 'ere? Has any of you seen a scruffy mudlark?"

There was a scatter of rough cries. "Go on, Jasper, give 'im a slice! Open 'is face for 'im! Nosy devil!"

"Does that satisfy you?" Jasper finished his bottle and smashed it into the gutter at Dick's feet. Broken glass scattered along the cobbles.

Keeping an eye open for treachery, Dick turned. "What d'you think?"

"The boy's here, I reckon," murmured his shipmate. "Inside the *Black Parrot*."

"And the mermaid," said Dick. "But nothing we can do right now."

Peter eyed the gang that stood at Jasper's back. "First thing's to get out of this alive and beat it back to the ship. Decide what to do then."

Dick turned back to face Jasper. "All right, maybe you're telling the truth. But do us lads a favour, will you. Keep your eyes skinned. If the boy turns up, send him back safely. He's done no harm to you. We'll pay you back sometime."

"He's frightened, Pa!" Albert tugged his father's sleeve. "Look at 'em – they're yellow!"

"That's right, son. An' they've got cause to be!"

A growl rose from the cut-throats who crept closer. There was a whisper of steel and cocking pistols.

"All right, salty sailor, we 'eard you. Now go on, get out of it – while you've got the chance!" Emboldened by his support, Jasper stepped forward. "If the boy turns up – *if*, mind – we'll pack 'im off with a flea in 'is ear, all right? Now push off! Sling your 'ook! If you're not out o' this square by the time I count to ten, I'll set the mob on you! One – two –"

The two sailors backed away.

"Four – five – six –"

At the sight of their retreating figures the gang from the *Black Parrot* could resist no longer. A scatter of pistol shots sent lead balls whistling about the sailors' heads.

With a bloodthirsty howl the outlaws charged. Knives and cutlasses flashed in the fading light. Dick and Peter fled headlong. Across the cobbles they sprinted and down the nearest alley. Jasper Dredge and his ruffians were left behind. Looking back, the sailors saw them clustered at the edge of Hangman Square. A few last threats and pistol shots rang out; spent bullets whined harmlessly from wall to wall.

Thrusting their cudgels into belts, Dick and Peter turned for home. A wind blew gustily and tossed their hair. Far off, beyond the river and forest of factory chimneys, a bank of storm cloud, black as ink, rose from the west and obliterated the setting sun.

"We got to get rid of 'im!"

"Yeah!"

It was early evening. Jasper and Albert lounged by the fire in the bar-room of the *Black Parrot*. The inn was quiet. Sammy, the treacherous pot-boy, cleaned the hearth at their feet.

"That young sailor's not to be trusted. Tanner to a guinea him and that shipmate are plannin' something right now." Jasper was halfway through another bottle. He took a long swig and grinned with wet lips. "But we'll be ready for 'em!"

"What are we goin' to do, Pa? Will there be *blood*?"

Since the matter of Silas's knife, Albert had taken a

delight in tormenting the pot-boy. Seeing him bending, he kicked him with the heel of his boot, head-first into the cinders.

"Oh, dear!" He laughed. "Fallen again?"

Spitting ashes and brushing dust from his smock, the pot-boy regarded him with loathing.

"Fetch us a goose-leg, Sammy," Albert said. "An' quick about it." He stretched his legs to the crackling logs. "What are you goin' to do, Pa? Tell us now."

"Well, the first thing's to get rid of that dratted boy. Don't matter too much if they find the mermaid – nothin' they can do about that. Finders keepers. But the boy..."

Albert pondered. "How do you mean, Pa – *get rid of 'im?*"

"What do you think I mean?"

"I get you!" Albert gave a slow smile of anticipation. "That's rich! When, Pa?"

"Sooner the better. Why not tonight? After we bring the mermaid back. Some time after midnight, when the square's empty. No point in advertisin' it."

"What are we goin' to *do* with 'im?"

A squall whined in the chimney and flung raindrops against the window.

"You remember that intruder we was talkin' about? An' what Cut-throat Frenchy done to Squealer Pigg? I reckon it's time we christened that knife o' yours, don't you? From the sound of things it's goin' to be a wet night. Dump his body down that drain in the square, let the flood-water carry 'im away. He'll be down-river an' half a dozen miles out to sea by morning."

"That's smart!" Albert fingered Silas's knife and thought about it. "That's keen! Who'll do it, Pa, you or me?"

A clock chimed above the bar. All in black, a highwayman primed his pistols, checked his mask and blood-crusted sword, and left the room.

"Another 'alf-hour it'll be time to take the mermaid out," Albert said.

"How much've we made so far?"

"Shall I count it again?" Albert said.

"Yeah, you do that, son. Meanwhile," Jasper took a last mouthful from his bottle and set it beside his chair, "I'm goin' to have a few minutes' shut-eye."

It was the evening hour when the *Black Parrot* began to stir. Villains arrived and villains departed. Now cut-purses and fingersmiths slipped through the streets, pockets heavy with the day's takings. Now grave-robbers set off into the night, shovels over their shoulders, cart-wheels wrapped in straw. Now coiners emerged from their dens; painted women made their way through the twisted Alleys; burglars and smugglers fortified them-selves against the evening cold.

Steadily the bar filled. Albert collected the money-bag

from its hiding-place and snatched the roast goose-leg from the pot-boy's hand. Munching greasily, he tipped the money into his lap and began counting it with fat fingers. The chink of coins and Jasper's loud snores rose against the growing hubbub of the evening.

Chapter Eleven

Midnight in Hangman Square

In the mouldy cellar beneath the *Black Parrot* the day passed slowly. No autumn breeze, no sunlight filtered from the streets above. Dick and Peter came and went unseen. The rattle of pistol shots in Hangman Square was remote as the tap-tap of the death-watch beetles in the timbers of the ancient inn.

And then it was evening – Saturday evening, a time of high spirits and riotous behaviour. With ropes and rough hands Ooli was bound and carried off to be shown in the bars and inn-yards of the city. Left in the dark with his fearful imaginings, Silas lay close to Bosun and listened to the sounds of revelry in the bar-room overhead. Thin fists clenched, he racked his brains for some means of escape. By candle-light he had searched every centimetre of the cellar walls and found the stone solid. The door was so stout it might have been fashioned for a prison rather than a cellar. When Jasper and Albert took Ooli away their thick frames had filled the entrance, there was no way past. Shivering with the cold, he huddled inside his sack and could think of nothing.

It was midnight when they returned. Footsteps descended the stairs and advanced along the passage. Heavy with rum, Jasper was singing. Keys rattled in the lock and the door swung open. Silas shaded his eyes against the brilliance of the lantern. The massive silhouette of Jasper stood in the entrance. Ooli was in his arms.

"Right, there y'are." He dumped her on the wet floor. "Your cell-mate can untie you again." His voice was thick. "Make use of 'im while you can."

"What do you mean?" Silas ran forward and caught him by the sleeve. "You're not taking her away?"

"Let go o' me!" Jasper shook him off like a troublesome terrier. "Get your 'ands off! I'm warnin' you!"

It was raining. His sleeve was wet, raindrops scattered from his hair. He retreated into the corridor.

"Not 'er – you!" Albert said with relish. "It's you we're takin' away – or puttin' away, more like. Kkkkk!" He drew a finger across his throat. "Your sailor pals have been pokin' their noses where they're not wanted."

"That's enough, Albert," said his father. "Come on, lock up."

"Jus' coming." He grinned, showing his dirty teeth. "Another hour – when things get a bit quieter, like – me an' Pa'll be down to see you. All right?"

The door banged shut, keys jingled, footsteps receded along the corridor.

Silas hammered on the boards.

"Albert Dredge! Albert Dredge! Let us out!"

There was no answer. The sounds of their jailers faded up the cellar stairs.

Silas loosened Ooli's ropes. Gently he rinsed her and they retreated to the overturned barrels. What did Albert mean: *It's you we're puttin' away! Some of your sailor pals have been pokin' their noses where they're not wanted!* What had been happening?

An hour passed. Gradually the noise in the bar-room quietened. Bosun whined and crept closer, touching Silas with his nose.

"Listen!" Ooli sat up. "Someone's coming!"

Silas strained his ears but could hear nothing. Then a faint chink of metal sounded at the far side of the door. He threw off his sack and ran across the floor. Softly a key was slipped into the lock. It did not fit. Another took its place. With a *cl-ick* the heavy lock snapped back. The key was withdrawn. The door creaked open a hand's width. There was a rustle of clothes as someone crept away. Silas peeped through the gap. In stocking-feet Sammy, the pot-boy, headed for the stairs.

"Pssst! Hey!"

Sammy spun round in alarm.

"What's this?"

"Scarper, quick!" The pot-boy was terrified.

"What, are you letting us out?"

"Yeah."

"Is the road clear?"

Sammy nodded. "But get a move on!"

"Really – or is this another trick?"

"No, no trick. That Albert Dredge, I 'ate him! You done me no 'arm. I played a rotten game on yer – but I wouldn't kill yer. That's what they're plannin' in there. They're a lot o' murderers!"

Silas's neck prickled. "What about the back door?"

"I'll open it. I've got to go! If they catch me down 'ere I'm done for an' all." On silent feet he flitted up the stairs.

Silas turned. "Ooli! Here, quick!"

She slithered across the floor, Bosun at her side.

"The pot-boy's given us a way out, but we've got to be quick – and quiet."

He pushed the door wide. Light filtered from the corridor above. As silently as possible they made their way up the passage and began to mount the cellar steps. Ooli's tail rustled on every tread. Bosun panted and slapped away saliva with a wet tongue. "Sshhh!" She held a hand over his muzzle.

A single voice came from the bar-room. There was a drunken guffaw.

They froze, then continued to the top of the steps. The bar entrance was right beside them. With thudding hearts they turned down the long corridor.

The door to the yard stood ajar. There was a flash and rumble of thunder. A steady hiss and splash from the gutters told them it was raining heavily.

As they passed a kitchen doorway Silas stifled a cry and started back. Jasper Dredge sat at one of the tables. A centimetre at a time he peeped into the room. A snore revealed the truth. Conquered by rum, Jasper was sound asleep. His massive red head rested upon an arm. Loose fingers curled round a half-eaten pie. Fat legs were buckled beneath his chair.

The bag of money hung at Jasper's waist. Silas gnawed his lip.

"You go on," he whispered. "I'll be right behind you."

He had left his clumsy boots in the cellar. Barefoot he tiptoed into the room. Reeking of sweat and spirits, the snoring giant sprawled beside him. A bottle lay on its side. His big dagger was stabbed into the table-top. His boots were loosened. Silas hesitated, then going on one knee he knotted together the trailing laces. With gentle fingers he removed the money-bag from Jasper's thick belt.

Ooli and Bosun waited at the entrance. Silas flitted the length of the corridor and joined them in the yard. He pulled the black door shut behind them.

The mermaid turned her face to the rain. Water from a drain-pipe splashed over her tail.

"Wonderful!" She looked up at Silas. "Now we are outside – how do we travel? I cannot run like you."

Silas extinguished the lantern at the inn door. "On horseback," he said. "Follow me."

Clutching the money-bag, he led the way across the yard. A horse whinnied in the stable. The doors stood open. He advanced into the animal-smelling darkness.

"Who's that?" a voice called threateningly. "Go on! Get out of it, you varmints – afore I set about you!"

Silas fled. At Ooli's side he crouched in shadow beneath a wall. The crabbed figure of an old watchman appeared in the stable entrance. This way and that he peered through the pouring rain but did not venture out. "Vagabonds!" they heard him mutter. "Thieving no-goods!" After a minute he went away again.

"Where now?" said Ooli.

Silas ran to the end of the stables. The rag-cart was gone. Quickly he searched the yard but it was nowhere to be found. Hair plastered to his head and trousers clinging, he returned to the mermaid.

"It's not there. But there might still be a way," he said uncertainly. "I thought about it down in the cellar."

"We must try!" Ooli hissed. "If we are caught again, then what that boy said to you – " her voice trailed away. "And I will die in some dirty cage! There are three of us." She patted Bosun's wrinkled head. "We can fight! I will *never* give in to that man, Jasper Dredge. He will have to kill me first!" Her nails dug through Silas's sleeve. "Now tell me, what must we do?"

Briefly Silas outlined his plan.

Her eyes glittered. "Yes," she said.

A stack of lopped-off branches provided them with sticks in case they had to do battle. Then, Silas leading, they crept from the inn yard.

At that hour of the night the square was deserted. No gas-lamps shone near the *Black Parrot*, the moon showed fitfully between ragged clouds. A flash of forked lightning split the sky above the river and was followed by a deep roll of thunder.

Silently the three made their way along the front of the inn, hugging the shadows, then ventured across the broad pavement. Silas felt very exposed. In Hangman Square, temporarily, the rain had ceased. Moonlight glinted on wet cobbles. Water ran musically down a broad gutter and splashed through an iron grid into the drains beneath. This was the place where Silas had skidded and fallen when Carver threatened him in the fog outside the *Black Parrot*. It was here the beggar's coins had scattered and fallen *plop* through the grid into water. It was a large grid, a manhole, which gave access to the underground network of great drainage channels that carried the water from the city streets.

"Keep a lookout!" Silas said.

Kneeling, he tugged at the iron bars, gritting his teeth with effort. Ooli lent her strength but it was no use, the grid was too heavy and firmly stuck.

"Stand back!"

Silas inserted the end of his stick between the bars and heaved. The stick bent. With all his weight he hung upon it. Abruptly the end of the grid shot up, slewed sideways, and fell to the cobbles with a metallic clatter.

They stared around. A thin figure appeared in an entrance. It was one of the scavengers who haunted the square, living off pickings from the villains in the *Black Parrot*. He gave a shout and started forward.

"Quick!" cried Silas. "Pull it aside!"

They tugged the heavy grid clear of the hole. Noisily it scraped over the stones. With a final clang it fell.

Summoned by the disturbance, other figures were appearing. Tattered skeletons of men, human jackals and vultures, black-toothed and claw-handed, they scrambled over walls and through broken railings.

"Stop them!" Raucous cries pierced the night. "Help! Jasper! They're getting away!"

Bosun growled menacingly. Silas recovered his stick. "Hurry! You first!"

Roughly he helped Ooli to the gaping hole. Rainwater cascaded into the darkness. Tail-first she began to disappear, clinging to the foot-hoops with strong hands.

The first scavenger was upon them. Bosun sprang forward, snarling and biting. The scarecrow figure tried to beat him back. Another clutched at Silas with clawed fingers. He hit out with the stick. The man gave a cry and let go.

Lights had appeared at the windows of the inn. The door burst open.

More figures came running. Some carried lanterns. Left and right, biting and snarling, Bosun was a fury. Silas laid about him with the stick. The end was seized; violently it was wrenched from his grasp.

"Silas!" Ooli's voice echoed in the black tunnel. "The drain!"

He backed towards it. A hand caught him by the jacket.

"Oh, no you don't!" It was Albert Dredge. "Try to escape that way, would you!"

Silas swung the bag of money into the fat boy's face. With a howl of pain, Albert let go and clutched his nose.

Jasper came behind him. Roused from his drunken sleep and bruised where the knotted bootlaces had caused him a tumble, he was in a terrible rage. Like a madman he struck out in every direction with an axe and a soup ladle, the first weapons that had come to hand. Luckily the scavengers were nimble, for a single blow would have split open their heads like coconuts. With a roar he descended upon Silas.

"Ah! So it's you!" His mouth opened like a furnace. "Well, maybe this will save us a mite o' trouble!"

The crowd drew back. As Silas retreated towards the drain he trod on a corner of broken kerb. The sharp stone jabbed his foot and he stumbled. In a second Jasper was upon him, bowling him to the ground. In terror Silas looked up. The murderous figure stood above him, axe held high. Desperately Silas rolled aside. It was not enough. But even as Jasper began the fateful blow, Bosun sprang at him, tearing at his shoulder with the memory of a hundred beatings. The dog was so savage that Jasper, befuddled with rum, was knocked backwards into the running gutter.

Uttering hawk-like cries, several of the scavengers ran forward. Silas scrambled to his feet as they closed in upon him. With sudden inspiration he plunged his hand into the bag of money and flung a handful of coins into their faces. They stopped short. Silas flung another handful, and then the bag itself, high over their heads. Tinkling and winking, the pennies and shillings, half-crowns and sovereigns scattered across the cobbles. For an instant the scavengers hesitated, then with screams and outstretched hands they flung themselves upon the bright treasure, scrabbling like bedraggled crows, tearing at each other's clothes and eyes.

"Bosun!" Silas shouted above the tumult. "Here!" But the snarling, worrying dog took no notice.

Silas ran forward and hauled him off Jasper Dredge by the scruff of the neck. By force he dragged him to the gaping mouth of the drain.

"Down!" he shouted.

But Bosun was too excited and frightened. Right on the brink he planted his paws and struggled backwards. Seizing the dog in both arms, Silas pitched him down through the hole.

Jasper was too fat and drunk to rise quickly. Turning on one side, he flung the axe. Silas felt the blade whistle past his ear and heard it clatter away on the cobbles.

"Go on, you fools!" Jasper raged at his companions. "What's wrong with yer! It's only a boy! Grab 'old of 'im!"

Wolfish figures ran forward. There was no time to search for handholds. Feet-first Silas plunged into the darkness.

Chapter Twelve

Red Eyes and Rats

Luckily the drain was only three metres deep. Bosun landed on top of Ooli. Silas landed on both and twisted his knee. In a tangle of arms and legs they lay in the dark tunnel. Water from the rainstorm flowed past, bubbling and splashing, icy cold.

"Let me get at 'em! Give us that lantern!"

Abruptly the drain was full of light. Gazing up, Silas and Ooli saw the face of Jasper Dredge, twisted with fury.

"You'll not escape me that easy!"

He flung aside the soup ladle and hung the lantern from his belt. Then going on hands and knees in the square, he thrust a fat leg through the manhole and began to descend the iron hoops set into the wall.

"Hurry!" Slithering on hands and tail, Ooli set off along the tunnel. Bosun scampered at her side, tongue lolling from his big bulldog mouth. Silas tried to walk. His knee buckled beneath him. Gritting his teeth, he struggled after them.

Albert had joined his father underground. Lantern-light swung dizzily from wall to wall. Their shouts and oaths boomed down the long tunnel.

"Silas!" Ooli waited at a joining of waters.

"I can't go any faster," he called. "My knee! You go ahead."

Briefly, to ease the pain, he sank to the ground. In a moment the mermaid was at his side.

"The water here is deeper," she said. "I can almost swim. Put your arms round my neck."

Two rats, hump-backed, scuttled up the dripping walls and vanished into a crevice. Another swam ahead, sleek in the water. A fourth whiskery face watched with interest.

The drain-water splashed over Silas's face. Jasper and Albert were only a few paces away; their great frames filled the tunnel. He felt Ooli's tail lash once, twice. The walls slipped past.

"Come 'ere, you young dog!" Jasper roared. He broke into a clumsy run. "When I get my 'ands on you, I'll – " His foot skidded. Full-length he fell into the rippling water.

To and fro the strong tail swished at Silas's side. His legs trailed along the ancient brick channel. Jasper and

Albert tramped behind, their boots splashing in the flood.

Looking ahead, Silas saw a score of tiny red lamps, all in pairs. Like rubies they glowed in the Stygian darkness. They were rats, their eyes reflecting the lantern-light. He felt one scamper across his shoulder. Pouncing swiftly, Bosun snapped at three, four, and tossed their bodies across the drain.

They turned a corner and turned again. Pipes gushed from either wall. As rainwater drained from a thousand streets, the channels were deepening.

Ooli swam on. Shafts of light shone down manholes from the city overhead.

Knee-deep, Jasper and Albert swirled through the rising water.

Two hundred metres passed, four hundred, six hundred. Their pursuers were falling behind. Silas felt his heart lift.

Abruptly Ooli found the way blocked by a metal grille. Flood-water poured through, a smooth cascade, into a deep channel beyond. Silas tugged at the bars but they were set in stone. Lantern-light, glimmering round a bend in the tunnel, revealed there was no way past.

"We're trapped!"

"No." Ooli could see better in the dark. "Look."

They retraced their steps. Ten metres back a tributary drain ran in from the side, high up the passage wall.

They clambered from the streaming current. As yet only a trickle ran through this upper tunnel.

The rats, knowing that a flood was coming, had deserted their nests. As Silas crawled into the darkness, his fingers encountered furry bodies and long, naked tails. Sharp claws scuttled over his neck and ankles, squeaks were in his ears. Blindly he struck out. Ooli seized the rats in her clawed hands and flung them aside. Bosun barked and lunged.

Slowly they advanced. Silas's twisted leg dragged behind him.

"Sshh!" Ooli put a hand over Bosun's muzzle.

All three lay flat, heads lowered. Jasper and Albert were passing the tunnel mouth. Their legs surged in the water. In the flash of lamplight, Silas saw the seeping walls and gathering army of rats.

"Hey, look!" Albert was in the lead. "The road's blocked. Iron bars." He kicked beneath the water. "No way past. They must've cut off somewhere."

"Cut off! I'll cut 'em off, all right. I'll cut their lugs off for 'em! Their 'eads!"

The lamplight returned. Silas glanced along the low tunnel behind him. Two faces peered beneath a raised lantern, red hair plastered to their heads.

"Cor! Look at the rats!"

"Never mind the rats!" Jasper cuffed his son about the head. "What can you see?"

"I think – yeah, that's them, look!" Albert pointed. "Keepin' their 'eads down."

"Keepin' right company, an' all." Jasper felt at his hip but he had no weapon. "We'll get you yet! Albert, give us a leg up."

On hands and knees he struggled into the upper tunnel.

At once Silas and Ooli set off in the other direction. Now there was no water their progress was slower. Every stride brought the ruffians closer.

'We've got you now!" Jasper lurched drunkenly. "I'll stop your meddlin', boy! Very convenient down 'ere in the drains. An' you, Bosun, you treacherous dog!" Seizing a fallen half-brick, he slung it with all his might.

Silas ducked but his injured knee made him clumsy. The brick rebounded from the wall and struck him full on the temple. There was a nasty thud. Uttering a little cry, Silas fell senseless at the mermaid's side.

"Got 'im!" With shouts of triumph the Dredges hurried forward.

Ooli looked down – but Bosun reacted. In two leaps he was along the tunnel and sprang at his cruel master. Jasper cried aloud and put up his hands to defend his face. The lamp fell and was extinguished. In the darkness all was confusion.

Seizing her opportunity, Ooli caught Silas by an arm and began to drag him away. Progress was painfully slow. Behind her, the snarling Bosun kept Jasper and Albert at bay. Two minutes passed. Staring into the darkness she discerned the end of the tunnel. Water half a metre deep gushed down a drain beneath her.

"Bosun!" she called loudly. "Bosun! Come!"

With a last claw and bite, Bosun left the attack and scampered towards her.

"Good dog!" She patted the sodden coat. "Come, stay by me."

Holding Silas tightly, she slithered down into the current.

Side by side they continued – the mermaid, the ragboy and the ugly dog – deeper and deeper into the labyrinth.

Overhead, meanwhile, the stars had vanished behind an inky cloak of storm-cloud. Lashing rain, slanting past the streetlamps like rods of steel, beat on roofs and cobblestones. Drainpipes gushed across the pavements. Puddles leaped. Gutters overflowed. Bolts of lightning and crashes of thunder, tremendous in the open air, flickered down cascading grids and boomed through the miles of drains beneath the city streets.

Jasper's clothes were torn in a dozen places. Furiously he turned on Albert, who had beaten a safe retreat from the dog's attack.

"Coward!" he roared. "Cur!" Seizing his son by the scruff of the neck, he gave him a drubbing in the darkness.

Albert howled.

"Now, where's the lantern?"

It was found and with difficulty re-lit. Ill-tempered and smarting, the two Dredges set off again in pursuit.

Holding Silas's head above water, Ooli swam down tunnel after tunnel. Trotting in the shallows and sometimes swimming, Bosun kept pace alongside.

Little by little a terrible anger was growing in Ooli's breast – frightening feelings, cruel feelings, feelings that the little mermaid had never known before. Jasper Dredge and his son – who had soiled and imprisoned her, who had humiliated her before drunkards, who planned to kill Silas and had knocked him senseless with a brick, who had beaten Bosun, who carried knives and pursued them through drains – she burned to be revenged upon them. Her eyes stared and she blinked hard. Without her knowing it, a low crooning started in her throat, a note that Ooli had never heard, but some ancestral shred of memory recognized at once. It was the mermaid's song, the irresistible voice that for ten thousand years, since men first ventured on to the seas and oceans, had lured sailors to their death. It was the song of the Lorelei and the Sirens, the terrible, beautiful, treacherous song that promised paradise beyond whirlpools and happiness beyond foaming rocks.

The current was speeding up. Close to the tunnel mouth Ooli clung to a crack in the wall and gazed ahead.

Before them a great flood surged through the main city drain. More than two metres deep, leaping and racing, it carried the rainstorm from the streets to the broad brown river. Grasping Silas beneath the arms and Bosun by the scruff of the neck, she released herself into the torrent.

With strong sweeps of her tail she swam upstream to a crossroad of higher tunnels on the far side. Carefully she hoisted Bosun to safety – for if he had fallen he would have been lost for ever – and hauled Silas and herself up beside him.

Then, unable to help herself, for the first and only time in her life, Luiulia sang the mermaid's song – a haunting, thrilling melody that rose above the roar of the torrent and echoed through the maze of tunnels beneath the city.

At her side, Bosun shivered and raised his muzzle in a mournful howl.

Far off, a lantern moved in the darkness.

"Listen!" said Albert. "What's that?"

They stopped. Water foamed about their thighs. A distant boom of thunder reverberated through the passages. Then, faint as a gnat, the singing of the mermaid came to their ears. At once, though they did not know it, it was as if a spell came over them.

"This way!" Jasper cried. "The fool, she's letting us know where she is."

"Get off!" Albert struck at the rats that swam about his legs. "Get out of it! Ugh! They give me the creeps!"

At the end of the tunnel they halted.

"This way." Jasper turned to the left – then right – then left again.

Steadily the singing grew louder. They were bewitched. Albert forgot the rats. Jasper forgot his reason for pursuing the mermaid and the ragboy through the drains. All they heard was the singing, which drew them forward like men in a trance. Briefly their brutal lives were touched by beauty.

The singing mingled with a roar of water. Jasper listened, turning his head this way and that, then scrambled to an almost dry tunnel down which the music came most clearly. Wild hair brushing the roof he hurried along, followed by his beastly son. They broke into a crouching run. And half a minute later the dazzling beams of their lantern emerged above the brimming flood.

Directly opposite, Luiulia sat in the tunnel mouth. Long hair hung to her waist, her lovely tail trailed in the stream. Bosun pressed close. Silas lay on the other side, his head on her silver lap. His eyes were closed. Blood trickled from his temple. The ragged jacket and split trousers clung about his skinny frame.

Luiulia smiled. She was very beautiful. The lamplight touched her eyes with red. With slim fingers she combed her hair.

146

She was so close! Jasper stared across the metres of racing water. Albert's eyes were wide. They scarcely saw and certainly did not heed the army of rats which gathered at their backs.

Calm and yet wild as a sea-hawk, rejoicing in her revenge, Luiulia lifted her head once more. Her bewitching song, liquid and lovely and treacherous, rose above the flood.

Silas stirred. His eyes flickered open. As in a dream, he saw Jasper and Albert across the glinting current. The mermaid's hair was in his face, her voice was in his ears. With a groan he struggled to a sitting position.

"See!" Luiulia whispered. "See! They venture into the water."

On the far side of the tunnel Jasper stepped to the very brink of the torrent.

"They will be swept away! The water will choke them! Fish and crabs will pick their bones!" gloated the little mermaid. "I shall rid the city of this vermin!"

Silas felt a thrill pass through her slim frame as she raised her voice again in song.

"No!" He clung to her. "Ooli! We're safe here. Don't! They won't capture us again."

But Luiulia was blind to everything except her revenge. His voice scarcely reached her.

Albert advanced to his father's side. Their eyes were wide as the eyes of children.

"Come! Come!" the mermaid sang. "The water is lovely; the water will soothe you; the water is kind. In five paces you will be at my side." She smiled irresistibly and beckoned. "Come!"

"No!" Silas pressed a hand over her mouth. "No! Ooli, you mustn't!"

"Yes!" She tore his hand away. "Yes!"

Silas struggled with her. "No! Please! No!"

His blood streaked her arm. Her eyes rolled sideways.

"Don't!" Silas pleaded.

The singing faltered – then ceased. In the sudden silence the only sound was the hiss and gurgle of the current.

On the opposite side of the tunnel Jasper Dredge drew back from the brink. He passed a hand across his face. The spell was broken.

"Silas! Oh, Silas!" With a scream Ooli flung herself into the water. Her tail lashed. In a turmoil of foam she swam up and down the racing torrent.

When she returned she was weeping. Her eyes no longer gleamed red. Tears mingled with the flood-water on her cheeks. From head to tail she shivered and clasped thin arms about her shoulders.

"Look!" Silas pointed across the drain.

Behind Jasper and Albert, as far as the eye could see, the tunnel was massed with tiny red lamps. A solid carpet of rats, escaping from the flood, pressed about their legs and climbed the ancient brick walls. There were so many that in places they crawled on each other's backs, for the tunnel could hold no more.

Before the Dredges lay the leaping current; behind was the army of rats; and beyond the drains were filling. Already some were flooded to the roof. Slowly the rats crept forward. A hungry squeaking filled the air.

Silas's blood was chilled at the sound.

Albert turned and saw them. He gave a cry of fear. At the same moment one of the rats ran up inside his trouser leg. Frantically he struck at it. Another, lean and ragged, sprang at Jasper's knee. Quick as a flash it scuttled up his clothes and bit him on the hand. The fat ruffian shouted with shock – and dropped the lantern! Briefly it fell, bounced on the brink, and was plucked away by the surging water.

Instantly the scene was plunged into darkness. It might have been a signal for which the rats were waiting. The squeaking grew louder. Jasper and Albert cried aloud.

"So, they have their reward!" hissed Ooli.

Silas was horrified. "Will the rats –" He could not say it.

"Who knows? They might find a way back."

"In the black dark?"

"They would have killed you – both of us! It is what they deserve!" She caught Silas by the hand and grabbed

Bosun once more by the scruff of the neck. "Come! We must leave. The tunnel is filling. Hold tight!"

She slid from her seat, pulling Silas and Bosun behind her. Instantly the icy flood plucked them away, rolling and bumping in the darkness. Briefly, as his head rose above the water, Silas heard the shrieks of the Dredges, echoing down the long tunnels. Then the torrent washed over him, bearing him onwards, ever onwards, beneath the streets of the sleeping city.

Chapter Thirteen

Dawn Raid

For a mile the current swept them along. As storm-water gushed from the streets above, the flood swelled. On rising waves Silas's head bumped the top of the tunnel. Alone he would have drowned, but Ooli held him fast in the darkness.

At length a tiny blue-grey arc appeared ahead. Rapidly they drew close. With a rush the torrent swept them out into the brimming river.

After the black confines of prison and the drains, the fresh air and broad night sky hit them like an explosion. Silas and Ooli shouted aloud.

On both sides of the river, in places two abreast, lay the great sea-going ships. Their rigging formed a forest against the twinkling gaslights of the city. The storm was moving away. Last flashes of lightning and rumbles of thunder came from further down the coast. A veiled moon showed through gaps in the cloud.

The place where the drain ran into the river was upstream, too far from the rag-and-bone yard for Silas to walk with his injured knee. Ooli helped Bosun ashore. Unaccustomed to such freedom, he sniffed and scampered along the riverbank, while Silas and the mermaid swam downstream beneath the city bridges.

A night-watchman stared as they passed far below.

In time they came to the broad harbour. The salt water – for the tide was high – made Silas's eyes sting. Half a mile distant the lighthouse at the end of the breakwater flashed against the night.

"Look!" Silas pointed. "There's the *Morning Star.*"

Ooli swam beneath her towering black plates and past the *Sea Urchin*, still bobbing on a line from the bow.

"I'd better go aboard and tell Dick we're back," said Silas. "I'm sure he's been out searching for us. And some of the gang from the *Black Parrot* might come looking for Jasper." He scrambled from the water on to a flight of weedy steps. "Will you stay there?"

"I won't go far." In sudden high spirits Ooli flipped from the water like a dolphin. Hanging on to a trailing rope, she watched Silas climb the steps and limp along the deserted quay.

Bosun joined him and jumped up to be patted. They continued to the gangplank.

"Hey, Silas! Where have you been?" Billy, the young

deck boy, was night watchman. Following the party aboard ship that night, his eyes were smudged with tiredness. Families and friends had long departed; sodden streamers lay on the deck.

He accompanied Silas to the fo'c'sle.

"In the cellar of the *Black Parrot* – we guessed as much. How did you get away?" Dick Chatham blinked in the lamplight, his hair tousled with sleep. "Come on, young Silas, you look frozen to the marrow. Wring your clothes out and warm yourself at the stove. Get a mug of hot cocoa down you. Then tell us all about it." He patted Bosun. "Where did you get the dog?"

The fo'c'sle was half full. Though most of the crew were on leave, many had stayed aboard after the party. A few were suffering the effects of too much grog, but the rest gathered round or listened from their hammocks as Silas told his story. When they heard about the mermaid they ran out on deck in their shirts and drawers.

Ooli waited in the moonlight. The sailors gathered along the rail. The little mermaid did not like being stared at but the sailors were friendly. They called and she waved back, then sank from sight and surfaced in shadow beneath the stern of the next ship.

They returned to the fo'c'sle, rubbing bare arms and legs, for the night was chill. Dick dressed and Silas pulled on his wet trousers and jersey.

"Well," Dick thrust a club through his belt, "I'll take

young Silas back to his grandfather and keep a lookout. Some of those thugs from the Alleys might turn up." He looked round at his shipmates tucked up in their warm hammocks. "I'll see you slugabeds in the morning."

"Right-oh, Dick." A young sailor yawned. "Blow out the lamp when you go."

They descended to the quay. Silas leaned above the lapping tide.

"Ooli, what about you? Are you coming up to the house?" He glanced at his companion. "Dick'll carry you."

"No, I'll stay down here with Bosun." Her hair floated wide. "It's safer. He'll be good company. I'll catch him a big meal of fish; dogs like raw fish."

"What about tomorrow?"

She thought. "I'll be in the harbour at dawn. But when the men start work I'll swim round to –"

"There won't be any work tomorrow," Dick said. "It's Sunday. Everyone'll be at church or having a lie-in."

"Well, I will be here." She looked at the *Sea Urchin* rocking behind her. "I might rest for a while in your boat."

"Take care, lass," Dick called down. "The ones who had you prisoner – they're a rough lot."

"I know – but they will not catch me a second time. Come on, Bosun."

With a leap and a splash she set off down the harbour. The yellow mongrel looked at Silas with his head on one side, then gave a joyful bark and scampered in pursuit. In a minute they were gone behind the stacked cargo and lines of moored ships.

With Dick at his side, Silas limped barefoot across the broad quay and climbed the cobbled street to his home. His knee burned. His broken boots lay in the cellar below the *Black Parrot*.

The gate to the rag-and-bone yard stood open. Much had been stolen in the days he was away. Softly he pushed open the door of the house and entered the living-room.

His grandfather lay on the old settee. He was sound asleep. In the grate the fire lay dead for the coal was exhausted. Silas glanced at the grandfather clock. It was a little after three o'clock in the morning.

"Poor old chap," Dick said. "Just look at him – worn out."

At the sound of voices and draught of colder air, Old Silas stirred. His eyes opened.

"Silas, boy! Is it you?"

Close to tears his grandfather hugged him, then held him at arm's length to examine the swelling on his forehead. A sudden spasm of coughing left him struggling for breath.

"Come on, Granda!" Dick said cheerily. "Let's pull

you closer to the fire. Now, what can we do about firewood?"

In five minutes he had smashed up an old table in the yard and chopped it into manageable lengths. Silas cleared the ashes from the hearth. A cheery blaze sprang up the chimney.

"Put on the kettle, Silas. What food's in the house?"

Peter's cake stood untouched on the table but the bread-tin and shelves were empty. Dick felt in his pockets and found a silver sixpence. Ignoring the hour, he hammered on Granny Porter's door and returned with a big loaf, butter and cheese, a jug of milk and several spoonfuls of tea in a screw of paper.

Soon, toasting their hands at the flames, Silas and his grandfather were tucking into plates of wholesome food and scalding cups of tea as Silas told his story for the second time. While Dick was out, he had changed into an old nightshirt of his grandfather's. His sodden clothes, twisted with wringing, steamed on the pulley overhead.

The cake and loaf were cut and cut again.

With a welcoming *miaow*, Sweep sprang on to Silas's lap and rolled on his back. Silas tickled his stomach and Sweep caught his fingers with needle claws.

"Come on," Dick said at length, for Silas's eyelids were closing. "It's time you were both in your beds. I'm going to keep watch down the street so you've nothing to fear, no one's going to surprise you... Don't argue, it's all decided. Bolt the gate and lock the door, make sure all the windows are fastened – then off you go."

Having borrowed a blanket, the young sailor retreated a short way down the street towards the harbour. In the shelter of a low wall he made himself as comfortable as stone and the November night permitted. It was a spot from where he could see the gate of the rag-yard plainly and keep an eye on the gaslit streets around, yet remain unobserved himself.

Silas dropped the locking-bar in place, turned the key in the back door and thrust the bolts home, then went through the house checking that every window was secure.

"'Night, Granda," he called sleepily.

"Goodnight, Silas, boy. I'm that pleased to have you home! Sleep well."

Silas mounted the steep stairs to his bedroom, pulled the curtains to shut out the street, and climbed into bed. His knee throbbed. With a silent leap, Sweep landed on the foot of the bed and trampled a comfortable hollow in the blanket. Silas reached down and rubbed his silky ears. With a loud purr Sweep responded. Then Silas turned on the pillow and tugged the bedclothes about his neck. A minute later, despite all that had happened, he was sound asleep.

But for a long time, in a room along the threadbare

landing, his grandfather lay awake. Staring into the darkness he thought about Dick Chatham out there in the cold, and the danger from which Silas had so recently escaped. He blamed himself. He was not so very old. If only he had his *strength* again!

For a time it rained, then the clouds rolled back to a clear and starry sky. Slowly the moon moved above the chimneys. Far and near, with chimes and bells, the city clocks marked the passing of the night. Dick drew his knees to his chin and twitched the blanket close.

A little before dawn it grew colder. Dick took pipe and tobacco from his pocket and struck a light. "Ahhh!" He sighed softly as he drew in the fragrant smoke and returned the equipment to his pocket. Contentedly he puffed and curled a hand round the warm bowl of his pipe. A thin trail of smoke rose above the wall.

He heard nothing, he saw nothing. Dick Chatham was a brave and simple young seaman, unused to the cunning of the streets. The first he knew of intruders was a hand clapped suddenly across his mouth, a knife pressed to his windpipe, and a harsh whisper: "Struggle an' I'll slit yer throat!"

Cloaks and black leggings were all about him; there was a smell of rum and sweat. In a moment he was gagged, a filthy cloth was bound across his eyes, and he was trussed hand and foot. Helpless as a bullock at the slaughter, he was dragged on his back through bushes into a hidden corner. A tight rope tethered him by the neck to a drainpipe bracket low in the wall.

"That'll do," came the harsh voice. "He'll not get loose; if he struggles, he'll choke! Now for young Silas Fisher an' that mermaid. If there's a lookout, they must be back."

On soft feet the company flitted up the street and stopped at the wall of the rag-and-bone yard.

"The gate's shut. 'Ere, Midnight Charlie, you're a burglar. Nip over that wall an' let us in."

In a moment the man was atop the brick wall. Silent as a shadow he dropped inside and lifted the bar of the gate. Black figures ran into the yard.

"Right! Now for the 'ouse!"

The door and windows were securely fastened.

"Sorry." Feely Sly, the top safe-breaker in the city, returned his tools to the bag. "Can't do nothin' when the bolts is shot."

"Just 'ave to smash a winder, then." The leader gestured with a thumb. "Some of you keep an eye on the street. Make sure *no one* gets out, right!"

Several of the gang ran back through the gate.

A small pane of glass was covered with treacle and brown paper.

"Give us room!"

With one blow of an elbow the window shattered. The paper was withdrawn, stuck all over with fragments of glass. A hand reached through and unfastened the window catch. The window slid up. Midnight Charlie threw a long leg over the sill, and a minute later the door swung open.

In his room at the head of the stairs Old Silas woke with a start and sat up in bed. He was sure he had heard something – but all was silent. He strained his ears. No sound came from Silas's room. The street was quiet. Out on the landing Sweep mewed suddenly and scampered across the floorboards. Uneasily he sank back on the pillows.

In his bedroom next door Silas never stirred. Dead to the world, sleeping the sleep of the young and exhausted, he heard nothing.

Abruptly his door crashed wide. Feet tramped heavily, there were loud voices all about him. With a cry he woke, eyes pricking in the sudden brilliance of a lamp. Next door his grandfather was shouting. Black figures came swarming into his room. Silas jumped from his bed and stumbled in the long nightshirt. A giant figure picked him from the floor and flung him back on the tumbled sheets. In terror, as in a nightmare, he found himself staring straight into the face of Jasper Dredge.

Jasper was scarcely recognizable. His face and ears were scarlet and swollen, bitten in fifty places by the rats. His hands, too, were bitten, and his clothes fluffed out in tufts from shoulder to boot. His hair and beard were wild, his eyes glared.

But he was alive. Luck had been with the Dredges. After a horrific struggle down the rat-filled tunnel they had descended into a broader channel and – with the creatures still clinging to their jackets – turned upstream against a thigh-deep current. Within a hundred metres a glimmer of light had led them to a manhole and escape to the city above.

Now, accompanied by a dozen cut-throats, thieves and other villains – all those of the *Black Parrot* gang who were not too drunk on Saturday night – he had come for revenge.

Albert stood at his father's side. He was in an even worse state, for his skin was young and he had no beard to protect his cheeks. Rats' droppings were in his hair. His red neckerchief hung in tatters. Bitten wrists protruded from his sleeves.

"Ahhh!" Jasper cried with pleasure. "We 'ave you now! Where's that mermaid? Quick, or I'll cut your arm off!" He drew his rusty sword.

"She's gone!" Silas answered bravely. "Away back to sea where you'll never catch her, Jasper Dredge!"

"What if I don't believe you, boy?"

Jasper raised the sword as if to carry out his threat – then let it fall.

"Fetch 'im downstairs. 'Im an' that coughin' wreck of

a grandfather. Per'aps the old man'll see sense where the boy won't. An' search every last corner of this 'ouse for that mermaid. Rip it apart if you need to. My property, she is! An' I plan to 'ave 'er back!''

Rough hands seized Silas and dragged him down the stairs. His grandfather, white with rage, already stood in the living-room.

"By God, Jasper Dredge! If I was a fit man you wouldn't treat my house like this!" He struggled for breath.

"Tie them up, boys," Jasper said. "In them two wooden chairs. An' build the fire up – it's cold as charity in 'ere.'' He grinned cruelly. "Then them an' me's goin' to 'ave a little chat.'' With the tip of his sword he tickled Silas's ribs. "We've got things to discuss. 'Aven't we, lad!''

Chapter Fourteen

Albert

For two hours the young mermaid and the yellow mongrel with a bulldog head ranged the seashore. Ooli swam far out to sea, plunging through the clean waves. From head to tail she scrubbed herself with handfuls of weed to get rid of the last taint of prison and the city drains. Her hair streamed, her skin tingled, her tail shone silver once again. Bosun, meanwhile, ran about the moonlit beach and promenade, chased fishermen's cats and rooted beneath piles of rubbish, as happy as a puppy. Then Ooli caught a cod and two fine haddock – and for dessert, two crabs and ten scallops. Side by side they lay on the sand and gorged until their stomachs were full.

Contentedly they returned to the harbour. Giant stacks of cargo stood in the gaslight; the big steamers and sailing ships were tight at their moorings; a hundred barges and dinghies rocked on the tide. Bosun found himself a dry bed beneath a tarpaulin. Ooli slid from the water and made herself comfortable aboard the *Sea Urchin*, drifting beneath the bow and hanging anchors of the *Morning Star*. And there, for the brief remaining hours of the night, they settled down to sleep.

Up at the rag-and-bone yard, meanwhile, Jasper Dredge was in a rage. Ringed by crooks and desperadoes, he felt disgraced. None of his terrible threats – ropes, chains, knives, fire – could budge Silas from his story: Ooli had swum off to sea and was never coming back.

"An' I'm tellin' you I don't believe you!" The corners of his mouth were white with foam.

"Let me 'ave a go at 'im, Dad!" Albert interrupted eagerly. "I'll get it out of 'im!"

"Just a minute, just a minute! You bloodthirsty little 'ooligan!" Jasper pushed him back impatiently. "Now, one last time, young Fisher. Tell me – or I'll chop your grandad's 'ead off! An' this time I mean it! Where is she? Think carefully, now. I'll count to five. If you 'aven't told me by then – ! One, two, three..."

Old Silas interrupted. "Why won't you listen? She's gone – right, but maybe she's not gone yet. She's not here, anyway, you've searched every corner." Tied in the chair, hands behind, he coughed helplessly. "Where do you expect to find a mermaid – sitting by the fire?"

Carver, the sinister figure from outside the *Black Parrot*, gave Jasper a shove. "You wouldn't listen, would you. That's what some of us've been tellin' you from the start. Down at the harbour, that's where she is. In the water."

"Mebbe aboard that ship 'is mates come from," said a second man with a chalk-white face and leather gloves.

"Is that right?" Jasper seized Silas by the neck of his nightshirt. "Down at the 'arbour, is she?"

"No!" Silas rolled his eyes towards his grandfather. "I told you – she's gone!"

"Ah!" Jasper grinned and let go. "This time I *know* you're lying. Down at the 'arbour!"

"No, she's not!"

"Oh, yes, she is."

"Granda!"

"It's all right, boy. Ooli's safe where she is. They'll never catch her."

"That's what you think." Jasper stood back and sheathed his sword. "Us boys from the *Black Parrot* – no one's beaten us yet."

There was a growl of agreement.

"Armed police nor nobody," said Jasper. "We got ways, see – cunnin', clever. I can't see a skinny mermaid's goin' to give us much trouble. An' if we can't get 'er alive, we'll shoot 'er dead." He touched the pistol at his hip. "Yeah, even dead an' stuffed she's worth a packet. How many freak-shows an' museums do you think've got a real mermaid on display in their glass cases?"

He turned to Albert. "Cor, what a mess you look! Right, you stay 'ere an' keep an eye on these two while the rest of us go down the road."

"No, Pa! I want to go wi' you! Let 'Ooky Sharp stay. I want to see 'er struggle when you catch 'er again." He sniggered. "Or see 'er shot."

"Well, you can't. I want 'Ooky wi' me. Your job's to make sure these two don't escape. Right?"

With a sulky expression Albert gave way. Then his eyes fell on the remaining slice of cake and last of the bread and cheese on the table. He brightened. "Right, Pa. I'll 'ave a look round, shall I? See what I can find – not that there'll be much in this dump." He crammed his mouth with cake.

"Do what you like, son." Jasper rubbed his rat-bitten neck and winced. "Only I want this pair alive when I get back. You listenin'? Plans 'ave to be made."

The gang checked their weapons and buttoned their coats, preparing to leave.

"An' keep that fire built up," Jasper said. "It's cold as 'ell out there. I still ain't got warmed up after them drains."

With scowls and a clatter of boots on the bare floor-boards, they departed. The door shut, low voices came from the yard, they were gone. Silas and his grandfather were left alone with Albert.

"Well, isn't this nice!" He hacked an end off the loaf and spread it thickly with butter. "Jus' the three of us. Silas Fisher, the raggy rag-an'-bone boy, always pokin' his nose where it's not wanted. An' his scraggy grandad. Not long to go by the look of 'im. You know what, gramps, what I'm plannin' for you will be a real favour."

Silas struggled against the cords that bound him to the wooden chair.

"That won't do you no good. Expert at tyin' people up, my mates are." Albert took a bite from the block of cheese and threw it back on the table.

Old Silas saw the long teeth marks and smiled faintly.

"What you grinnin' at, Grandad?"

Old Silas nodded: "Rats like cheese."

Albert stopped chewing.

Silas regarded Albert's bitten face. "Rats like rats, too," he said.

Albert flushed, though his skin was already so inflamed that it was hard to tell. "You watch your lip!" he snarled and slurped a mouthful from the jug of milk. He looked round, from the hanging jumble on the beams to the chipped dresser and other scraps of furniture. "Right, where d'you keep the money in this flea-ridden 'ole? You skinny old misers always got a pile stacked away somewhere."

He hunted in the ornaments on the mantelpiece. One after another, as bowl and vase produced no money, he tossed them over his shoulder. Crash! Tinkle! Smash! Old Silas's little treasures, nicknacks that had belonged to his wife and mother, broke on the living-room floor.

"Stop that, Albert Dredge!" Silas cried. "Stop it! You're vile! Disgusting!"

Albert's thick lips parted in a smile. "Vile, is it? Disgusting! If I was you I'd watch what I say, young Silas Fisher. I'll remember them words."

Turning his back, Albert continued his search. Drawers splintered as they were flung aside. The poor contents scattered across the floor.

"'Allo, who's this?" He took up the small framed portrait of Silas's father.

"Leave that!" Silas cried.

"Oh, worth somethin' to you, is it?" Albert examined it closely. "Your old man? Croaked, is he? Right villain by the look of 'im."

Bending his head, he dripped spit on the glass and threw it into a far corner.

Silas could not speak.

The fire was burning low. Albert flung documents and anything else burnable towards the grate. Fresh flames leaped up the chimney.

His glance fell upon Sweep, who had gone to ground

beneath the big dresser. Eyes round and yellow, the little cat looked out on the scene of destruction.

"Well, what 'ave we 'ere?" Albert caught him with rough hands. Briefly he stroked the soft fur and looked at Silas. "Yours, I s'pose. Isn't that nice! Fond of it, are yer?" His fingers circled the black neck. "Who's a good puss?"

Sweep growled then gave a sudden squall and slashed Albert's hand with lacerating claws. Needle-sharp teeth sank into his thumb. With a cry Albert flung him aside. Twisting in the air, Sweep landed on four paws and retreated once more beneath the dresser. Savage as a fiend, ears laid flat and teeth bared, he stared up at his tormentor.

"What! I'll 'ave you!" Seizing the teapot and chipped plates from the table, Albert flung them at the little cat. Sweep fled around the room as the missiles exploded against walls and furniture. Suddenly ceasing, Albert examined his hand. "Never mind." He sucked away some drops of blood. "You'll get what's comin' to yer."

For several minutes he continued his search, but the remaining drawers and high ledges failed to produce the money he was convinced was hidden somewhere in the room. Silas and his grandfather watched helplessly as their shabby but respectable home was reduced to chaos.

Albert stood amid the debris. "Well, not much 'ere, is

there." His hot little eyes roamed the room and fell on the grandfather clock. "Ah! I wonder if it's 'idden in there. Yeah, the very place."

He wrenched open the door and rooted inside, but nothing was to be found. The pendulum clanged, the weights crashed to and fro. Something inside the works broke with a *twang* and the minute hand slumped to the half-hour.

"Oh dear! Worth a bit, too, by the look of it. Still, too 'eavy to cart all the way back to 'Angman Square."

With a heave Albert sent the beautiful clock smashing to its face on the floor. The case split, glass scattered across the boards. In a moment the work of Silas's great-great-grandfather was destroyed.

The crash made the room shake. An end of wood, flaming yellow, tumbled from the fire and lay smouldering on the hearthrug. Albert regarded it, then turned away. Slowly the flames died. Blue smoke drifted through the room and there was a smell of singeing.

"Now, where else?" Albert's eyes slid sideways.

Silas glanced towards the corner where his grandfather kept his wooden cash-box hidden beneath the floorboards. Albert intercepted his gaze. Silas looked away quickly.

It was too late. Quick as a weasel, Albert stared into the corner. It was empty. A broken umbrella stood against the wall. Heavy-footed, he ran across and seized it, shook it, opened it – but nothing was hidden inside. He flung the umbrella behind him and looked around. His hobnails clattered on the floorboards. Suddenly Albert understood.

"Aha! You crafty old devil!"

In a moment he was down on his knees. Now that he knew where to look, it was not hard to find the loose board. He prised it up and with a cry of triumph lifted out the box hidden beneath. With both hands he tugged but the lock was secure.

"No good askin' for the key, I s'pose?"

Old Silas regarded him silently.

"Ah, well! Makes no difference." He pulled Silas's sea-knife from his belt, inserted the blade and twisted. Still the lock resisted. He raised the box and smashed it down on the table – two, three times. With a crack and splitting of wood, the box broke open.

Papers and trinkets and the little washleather bag of money lay within. Greedily Albert untied the string. Two sovereigns and a few bright shillings fell into his palm. It was Old Silas's entire savings.

"That all? Still, better than nothin'." Albert dropped the coins into his pocket. "Lousy beggars!" Carelessly he threw the box and papers towards the fire.

"I'll get even with you one of these days, Albert Dredge!" Silas twisted his wrists.

"You think so? Reckon you got that long?" Albert

laughed. "I wouldn't take no bets on it. Me an' Pa's got plans for you an' the old man 'ere." Staring at Old Silas, he took another drink from the milk jug and another bite from the block of cheese. "Yeah, we'll teach you what 'appens to people who mess around with the Dredges. Trappin' us down in the drains wi' them rats – but we got out, didn't we! An' nickin' the money we earned, honest money, showin' that mermaid around; givin' it to the 'Angman Square scum! Yeah, an' gettin' Pa smashed up by that costermonger! Chuckin' rocks an' knockin' 'is 'at off! Young 'ooligan! But we'll show you, Silas Fisher. Jus' you wait!"

In a sudden fit of anger he knocked the milk jug across the room and threw over the table.

The violence seemed to pacify him.

Breathing heavily, Albert looked towards the window. "I wonder 'ow they're gettin' on down at the 'arbour." He opened the yard door. "Back in a minute. Don't go away." Sniggering, he crossed between the piles of junk.

A cold draught swirled round Silas's ankles. The sinking fire sucked and sparked in the chimney. It would soon be daylight; the first streaks of dawn showed red above the scrapyard wall.

Albert returned. "All quiet. Not a sound. I can just imagine 'em creepin' up on 'er. Springin' a trap. What a shock she'll get, eh?" He held his bitten hands to the warmth. "That sailor mate o' yours is quiet an' all. I wonder if they done 'im in on the way down. Maybe that's why Pa wanted 'Ooky Sharp with 'im."

Silas stared. Dick – and that little man with lank hair and a hook for one hand!

"Anyroad," Albert looked round the devastated living room, "I'm goin' down to join 'em. You pair'll be safe for 'alf an hour, woncha? Not miss me or nothin'? Not try t'escape?" He grinned and checked their cords, tugging the ends with vicious pleasure. "That's it, good an' tight. Don't reckon you'll get out o' them in a hurry. Now, what else?"

He swung the dusty shutters across the windows and secured the catch. "Never know who might come snoopin' round."

The door which led to the yard was sturdy. A large iron key protruded from the lock. He shifted it to the outside and tested it.

The inner door, which led to the hall and staircase, was flimsier, and although it had a keyhole, there had been no key for as long as Silas could remember. The door opened inward. Albert dragged the grandfather clock against it. It was not heavy enough. He looked round. The big Welsh dresser stood alongside. He squeezed his fingers behind the top and heaved. The solid piece of furniture rocked and crashed back upright. The crockery rattled. Setting his foot against the wall, Albert heaved again. In slow motion the dresser toppled.

Doors swung open, jugs and plates smashed to the floor. Briefly it balanced, then fell with a crash that shook the house. Albert grinned. Exerting his considerable strength, he dragged the dresser on top of the clock and jammed the inner door shut.

"That should do it." He straightened, tucking in his shirt, and looked around. "Now, what was it Pa said? Oh yeah, cold down there, keep the place warm for when he comes back."

A few sticks and a couple of logs still lay by the hearth. Albert set them in the grate and went out to the yard for more. There was a noise of breaking timber and he returned with arms full. Scraps of tar-paper made the flames leap. He stacked broken wood on top. Varnish blistered and flared.

"That should be enough." He dumped the remainder at one side and dusted his palms.

"Well, I'm off. You'll not be needin' the lamp – daylight soon." He blew it out. A demonic figure in the flickering light of the fire, he crossed to the door which led to the yard. "Won't be long. Bring you-know-who back to see yer – if she's still *alive*! Leave you to think about it, all right?"

He stood in the doorway, silhouetted against the red glow of sunrise. Abruptly, as if in response to his words, the sharp *crack* of a pistol came to their ears. It was followed by another, then a thin volley.

"Blimey! Sounds like they've shot 'er already!"

Albert swung away. The heavy door banged shut. The big key turned with a snap.

Chapter Fifteen

Ring of Flame

Tied up in chairs and wearing patched nightshirts, Silas and his grandfather were prisoners in their own living-room.

As Albert left, the sudden draught and slamming of the door shook the banked-up fire. The timbers collapsed; protruding sticks fell to the hearth. A blazing log bowled across the rug and struck a discarded drawer.

Silas struggled against the cords that bound him.

The drawer was split. Old papers spilled over the edge. They ignited. Dry rags and other debris were scattered around. In a minute a fierce fire had sprung up on the floorboards. Yellow flames leaped head-high, illuminating the room. Thick smoke coiled about the ceiling.

The heat scorched the side of Silas's face. The cords cut into his wrists.

"Help!" he cried, shrill as a seagull. "Help! Fire!"

But no sound penetrated to the street through the shuttered windows, the piles of scrap and high brick wall. In any case, the street was deserted.

The flames touched the clothes-pulley overhead. Silas's jacket and trousers were still wet but other garments were tinder-dry. All across the ceiling the open beams were hung like a forest with hanks of net, rags, old harness, ropes, twine, canvas, oilskins, broken chairs and other inflammable objects. A torn shirt burst into flame. In a moment the fire had leaped to a ragged bed-curtain and a bundle of rushes for repairing chairs.

"Granda!" Silas cried aloud. "Granda!"

"The glass, boy!" Old Silas kept his head. "The broken glass!"

"What?" Silas tugged and strained.

"The clock!" his grandfather cried. "There's glass on the floor behind you. Try to cut yourself free."

Silas twisted his head and saw the silver shards. With a lurch he flung himself backwards and crashed to the floor. His arms were beneath him. He struggled sideways and fumbled for the bright daggers of glass. A stinging pain, then another, told him that he had cut himself. Unheeding, he took the glass in his fingers and began to saw an edge across the tight cords.

Flames leaped along the beams. The ceiling was ablaze. All over the room burning rags fell to the floor.

More papers caught fire. A rotted lace tablecloth dropped like a bomb across the fallen dresser and grandfather clock; the dry wood burst into flame. Paint blistered and began to run. Blue flames flickered across the walls. Acrid fumes filled the air.

Silas and his grandfather coughed – and coughed again.

Terrified by the fire, Sweep dashed madly about the room but there was no escape. Yowling at the top of his voice, the little cat backed into a corner and stared at the flames that leaped up on every side.

Backwards and forwards, backwards and forwards Silas thrust the glass dagger across his bonds. Time and again he cut himself. The glass slipped in his fingers. He tugged at the cords – and sawed – and tugged again. Heat scorched the back of his nightshirt. Quick flames ran up the curtains at the shuttered window. A scrap of burning oilskin fell by his shoulder. Silas sawed on – and tugged – and choked on the smoke – and sawed again. Suddenly the cords parted. His hands were free. He cast the glass aside and leaned forward to loosen his feet. His fingers were red.

The cords fell slack. Silas kicked them off and scrambled to his grandfather's side. He was soon untied. Old Silas stood shakily and rubbed life back into his thin hands.

Silas ran to the back door and wrenched at the handle. In a frenzy he hammered on the boards.

"Help!" he screamed at the top of his rags-and-bones voice. "Fire! Fire!"

But no one came.

He ran to the window shutters. They were beyond reach. A tin of lamp-oil which stood on the ledge had spilled and ignited. Flame formed another curtain.

The room was like a furnace.

"Over here, boy!"

Old Silas stood by the inner door. In his hand was the long poker. In an extraordinary display of strength, the frail old man stood on the end with his bare foot and bent it into a hook. Shielding his face, he heaved at the dresser Albert had piled against the door that led into the hall. Tongues of flame singed his eyebrows. The blazing timbers skidded and stuck – skidded and stuck – then slid back. In a fountain of flame and sparks the grand-father clock collapsed beneath it.

The painted door was ablaze.

"My boots!" Old Silas struggled for air.

Dodging the fires which had broken out all over the floor, Silas ran to the hearth and carried them across.

"Water! Hurry!"

The water bucket stood beneath the window. Silas threw off the lid and ran back to his grandfather.

"Here!" The water was icy. Old Silas scooped handful after handful over his grandson's head and nightshirt, then did the same to himself. The wet cotton clung to their backs and legs.

Clutching the bent poker – weakness forgotten as he fought for their lives – the old man tugged at the shell of the grandfather clock. The blazing timbers broke. He hooked them across the floor. The smoking clock-face lay at the foot of the door.

Old Silas flung the last of the water over the burning panels. The door-handle sizzled. Snatching Silas's wet trousers from the pulley, he turned the handle and tugged. A corner of the dresser and broken boards from the clock prevented the door from opening. He heaved. A gap of half a metre opened. The flames surged. Beyond lay the black hallway.

"Through you go!"

"I can't!" Silas pointed.

The floorboards were smoking, patches glowed red. His feet were bare.

"Take off your nightshirt! Walk on that!"

Quickly Silas tugged off his wet nightshirt and spread it on the floor. Naked he looked behind him.

"Sweep! Where's Sweep?"

"Never mind Sweep! I'll look after Sweep!" His grandfather pulled the door as wide as it would go. "Go on, out! Quick! I can't hold it much longer!"

"Dad!" Silas dashed through the flames and snatched the picture of his father from the corner. Then like an eel, scorching his shoulder against the burning wood, he slid through the entrance into the hallway.

With a crash the door slammed shut behind him.

"Granda!" he cried. "Granda!"

Seizing the rug, he thrust it against the blistered varnish. The door cracked open. With all his strength Silas pushed. Something fell with a crash. The door opened wider. A gush of fire billowed through the entrance.

"Granda!"

But his grandfather did not appear. For a full half minute Silas waited, naked as a frog, scorched by the blaze. In tears he shouted again and again.

Then suddenly, arms about his face to ward off the flames, the old man ran from the inferno. His face was scarlet and streaked with black, his night-shirt steamed.

"Oh, Granda!" Silas flung his arms about his grandfather's chest.

A struggling bundle intruded between them. Hastily wrapped in Silas's wet jacket, Sweep complained loudly. He had not been easy to catch. Old Silas's hands were scratched as well as burned. Furious caterwauls rose against the roaring flames.

Silas ran across the hall and through the small lobby to the front door. "The key!" He looked round at his grandfather.

As always the front door, which they seldom used, was

locked. The key, for safety, hung on a nail in the living-room.

Old Silas stared back and shook his head.

Sweep struggled free. A paw, a black head, appeared from the soggy bundle. Not in the least grateful for his rescue, spitting and clawing, he jumped to the floor. For a moment he crouched, staring past their ankles into the blazing living-room, then bounded across the hall and up the steep flight of stairs.

"Come on, boy," said Old Silas. "He knows the way. Up you go."

Swirling smoke filled the hall, lit by the orange flames that seethed within the living-room and licked through the half-open doorway.

Limping with his sore knee, Silas scrambled up the stairs and ran along the landing to his bedroom.

It was dark. He flung back the curtains and loosened the catch of the window. As he pushed it wide a new sound rose from the hall below. The draught sucked flames through the living-room doorway. Roaring and hungry they surged to the banisters and began to lick up the uncarpeted staircase. He felt the sudden rush of heat.

His grandfather joined him and slammed the bed-room door. A handful of clothes that he had snatched from his own room trailed on the floor. He flung them from the window into the street.

The neatly-folded pile that Dick had brought lay on the chest of drawers. Silas threw them after.

"Give me a hand." Old Silas tugged the sheets and blankets from Silas's bed and began to knot the corners together.

Silas threw the end of the rough rope from the window and looked down. It reached nearly to the ground.

"That's enough, Granda."

As he turned back his eye was caught by a movement far down the street. Figures were chasing across the gaslit quay. Two were fighting.

There was time to see no more. Old Silas threaded the corner of the topmost sheet through the hinge of the window and knotted it securely.

"Down you go!"

Silas hesitated: would his grandfather be able to follow?

"Hurry up! Do you want us to be burned alive!"

The fire had reached the landing. A red glow shone beneath the bedroom door. Fingers of flame licked into the room.

Silas clambered to the sill. Below lay the broad pavement and cobbled street. He grasped the rope and lowered himself naked down the wall of the house.

He reached the ground. Unaware of the cold and wind, he stood back and looked up. Like a ghost his grandfather emerged from the window and clutched the knotted bedclothes in his burned hands. Slowly he began to descend, stick-like legs braced against the wall. Between his teeth, pulled from its spitty and broken frame, was the little portrait of Silas's father. Sweep clung to his shoulder, claws digging through the thin nightshirt. Smoke poured from the window. Flames flickered in the adjoining room.

"All right, Granda." Silas caught him. "You're down now."

Together they stood on the cold pavement. The dawn wind flapped the wet nightshirt about Old Silas's legs. His chest heaved but his eyes were bright. "Goodness!" Somehow he found the spirit to make a joke. "I haven't done that since I was courting your grandma." Then his face collapsed and he crushed his grandson against him and pressed his cheek to the top of the cold wet head.

Sweep sprang to the ground and dashed round the corner to what had always been the safety of the rag-and-bone yard.

"Come on, boy." Old Silas rubbed away his tears. "Better get dressed before you catch your death of cold – or they come to arrest you!"

They gathered their scattered clothes and followed Sweep to the privacy of the yard. Now the immediate danger was past, Silas felt the pain mounting in his knee.

The tall black gates swung loose. They walked through. The laboriously collected piles of scrap were silhouetted against a bright glow. Fire had devoured the shutters which covered the living-room window. The glass had exploded. Vicious flames coiled and roared within the house. A column of smoke poured into the sky.

"Well, that's that." Old Silas regarded it. "I wonder where we're going to live now."

The heat scorched them across the yard. Wet junk steamed in the early light.

Silas shook out the clothes Dick and his young brother had outgrown and pulled them on. They were thick and warm, the best he had worn for a long time. Their strangeness did not trouble him at all; Silas was used to wearing other people's cast-offs.

But Dick! Abruptly he remembered. Had Albert been telling the truth? Had Jasper taken the terrifying 'Ooky Sharp with him to – ? The thought was too horrible to contemplate.

Old Silas too had dressed. Sitting on the corner of a box and lit by the fire, cheeks whiskery and hair tangled, he stared towards the ruin of his home.

"Granda," Silas said tentatively. "I was wondering about Dick."

"Mm?" His grandfather raised his head.

"Dick," Silas said again. "D'you think Albert Dredge was telling the truth? Did Jasper take that man with him because – ?"

"No, he's not interested in a sailor. 'Sides, if he

harmed your pal he'd have all the sailors in port baying for his blood. No, it's Ooli he's after, the mermaid. In his hands she's worth money – she's a prize."

Silas thought of the figures he had seen running about the quay. Was Dick among them? Was Ooli safe? "D'you think I should go down and see what's happening?" He looked from the blazing house to his lonely grandfather.

"No, boy, you stay here. They're a dangerous lot."

"But they said they'd come back. And I want to find out about Dick and Ooli. I can keep out of sight." He avoided mention of his knee.

His grandfather sighed. "If you must, then. There's nothing for you to do here, anyway." Sweep emerged mewing from the broken remains of a cart. Old Silas took him on to his lap. "I'll not come with you. But take care! Stay well away from that murderous bunch down at the harbour. You hear!"

"Yes, Granda." Silas hesitated. "Will you be all right?"

"Why shouldn't I be?" Old Silas rubbed the cat's ears and smiled wanly. "What harm can I come to sitting at my own fireside?"

For the first time Silas realized what the loss must mean to his grandfather. He felt his own eyes prick with tears. Old Silas raised a hand and he squeezed it, then feeling like a deserter he limped from the yard.

As he looked back from the street a fiery glow shone above the scrapyard wall. Smoke and sparks whirled high into the air.

Chapter Sixteen

Revenge

It was a fresh morning. The heavy rainstorm had rinsed the air. In the silver dawn light the pavements shone, the horizon was clear.

But Silas had eyes for none of this. As he hurried down the road his knee hurt. What, he wondered, had become of Dick? What of Ooli? What was happening at the harbour?

Soon he reached the spot where Dick had said he would hide and keep a lookout. Silas looked behind the low wall. The space was empty. A broken tobacco pipe lay on the ground.

"Dick?" He called softly and then louder. "Dick!"

There was no response. On that Sunday morning the street was deserted, the curtains still drawn as the hard-working families slept late.

Then Silas heard a rustle. And a moment later a

bump. It came from a scrubby patch of bushes close by. Cautiously he approached. The sound was repeated. He heard a choking voice. "Nnnnn! Ugghhh!" Silas had no weapon. With a thin hand he pulled back a branch.

In a mouldering corner lay Dick Chatham, cruelly bound and gagged. His neck was tied to the bottom of a drainpipe. Water dripped into his hair.

"Dick!" Silas pushed through the bushes and crouched beside him. Fumbling in his haste, he tugged at the knots that held his friend captive.

Angrily Dick sat up and tore off the gag. "The dogs! The shore-rats! They jumped me. I never saw a thing." He rubbed life back into numb hands and legs. "But Silas, lad, you're safe anyway. What about your granda?"

Shielding his face, Silas returned through the bushes and looked up the street. Sparks and flame whirled from the upstairs windows of his home. Smoke drifted across the rooftops.

"What happened?" Dick was horrified.

"It's all right, Granda's safe." Briefly Silas told him about the fire.

"I'll never forgive myself," Dick said. "You could both be dead!"

"It wasn't your fault," said Silas. "It was Albert Dredge."

But Dick was troubled. "Your poor granda! Come on, we've got to help him."

Silas caught him by the sleeve. "No, look. There's Granny Porter – and the people from across the street."

The neighbourhood was wakening to the fire. Somebody was hammering on doors. Figures were emerging.

"There's nothing anyone can do," Silas said. "The house has gone." Blinking hard, he stepped into the road and looked down towards the harbour. "But what about Ooli? We might save her."

Dick joined him. The harbour was still: masts and funnels stood against the water, no boat moved on its rippled expanse. The quay too appeared peaceful. Then a distant figure dashed from behind a stack of cargo. He was pursued by another. Closer at hand a third man appeared. He stretched out an arm. There was a puff of smoke and a second later the crack of a pistol. A small figure aboard the *Morning Star*, whom Silas had not noticed, fell to the deck.

"That's my shipmate!" Dick started forward.

"Wait for me," Silas called.

"It's too dangerous. Besides, you've got a bad leg. You go back to your granda."

"No, I'm coming." Silas gritted his teeth and broke into a limping run. "Ooli's my friend. She's here because of me."

"All right." Dick waited for him to catch up. "But stay

out of the fighting. Here," he pulled the cudgel from his belt, "you'd better have this."

As they reached the foot of the road the harbour was hidden by a row of warehouses. They hurried between them and emerged on to the quay, seventy metres broad and nearly half a mile long: a warren of jetties, slipways, offices, cargo, docks, locks, ropes, nets, engines and gear.

At once they found themselves involved in the running battle that was in progress. Round the corner raced a withered man with staring eyes and hanging grey hair. It was 'Ooky Sharp. With a cry he collided headlong into Silas. But although he was in full flight he was no less vicious. His startled glance took in Silas and Dick. Baring crooked teeth, he lashed out with the hook that served him in place of a hand. Had it struck it would have ripped Silas to the bone. He jumped back and the next moment 'Ooky was gone, scurrying towards the passage between two warehouses. The shadows swallowed him up.

The next second two young sailors came tearing round the corner in hot pursuit.

"Did you see – ?"

Dick pointed and they ran on.

Briefly Silas and Dick watched them go then continued to the strip of open quay between the stacked cargo and the ships. On the cobblestones at their feet Silas saw spots of blood.

A short distance away two older sailors – one with a sword, the other with a batten of timber – were engaged in a life-or-death struggle with the ferocious Carver. His cloak billowed, steel clashed and sparks flew as he hacked and thrust. But he was outnumbered, step by step driven back against a stack of bales. The sailors came at him from both sides. Suddenly darting inside the reach of Carver's sword, the sailor with the batten swung a punch that nearly took the head from his shoulders. His legs buckled, the great sword fell from his hand and the murderous Carver dropped senseless at their feet. The panting sailors stood for a moment then clapped each other on the back and stooped to tie his wrists and ankles.

Far along the quay a dark figure, pursued by one in white, fled across a walkway. The sailor, fleeter of foot, overtook the villain swiftly and after a brief tussle flung him headlong into the deep water of a lock. The shrieks of the drowning man rose on the air. The sailor stretched a piece of timber towards him.

Silas looked up at the *Morning Star*. On the foredeck Billy, the young deck boy, pulled himself to his feet. He had been shot in the upper arm. His hanging hand was scarlet. Painfully he made his way to the top of the gangway. Seeing Silas, he managed a faint smile and raised the other hand.

At the foot of the gangway, guarded by an armed

seaman, lay three scowling ruffians clothed in black. Their weapons had been removed, their hands and feet were tightly bound. Carver, regaining consciousness, was dumped among them.

"Hey, Dick!" One of the sailors greeted them. "Where've you been? You missed the fight."

Dick outlined what had happened.

Their lively expressions were replaced by concern. "Aye, we saw the fire. Didn't know it was young Silas's home though."

They looked above the warehouses, up the steep street that rose from the docks. A small crowd had gathered at the rag-and-bone yard. Smoke and flame poured from the windows of the house. As they watched, the roof collapsed. A volcano of fire erupted above the housetops and flung sparks high into the sky.

"Oh, no you don't!" While their attention was distracted, one of the captives had slid a knife from his trouser leg. Dick plucked it from his fingers.

"Damn you, sailor!" The man spat up at him.

Dick checked his ropes and turned away.

"Why don't you and Silas keep an eye on this lot?" The guard poked them with his stick. "Then we can go and join the others."

"Where are they?"

"Hunting down the rest of these black rats."

"What, everybody?"

"Aye, those of us who slept aboard. Billy's the only one left. It's been quite a battle."

"A nasty lot," added a shipmate. "But we out-numbered 'em. Come down before dawn to put a rope on that mermaid. Poor Billy was asleep on the gangway – no wonder after all the grog he drank at the party. But she heard 'em all right. Sleepin' in Silas's boat. Give the alarm."

"Is she safe?" At last Silas had a chance to ask his question.

"She can look after herself, that one. Aye, she's safe enough. They took a few pot-shots at her, mind. She's somewhere in the water there."

Silas looked down but the surface was unbroken.

"About a dozen of them an' twenty of us," the sailor went on. "We only got these four, the rest run off. The boys are out there now, somewhere, tryin' to round 'em up."

"What about their leader, Jasper Dredge?" Dick said. "And that son of his, Albert?"

"Dunno. We was talkin' about that. There one minute an' gone the next when they saw the battle was turnin' against 'em. The quay was full o' people, mind – fights all over. Charlie, here, went huntin' for 'em but they'd gone. Must've scarpered when we wasn't lookin'."

Dick hitched his tarry bellbottoms and felt for his pipe but it wasn't there. He remembered.

"Aye, all right, boys. Off you go and join the others. Silas can keep an eye on this lot and I'll have a look at young Billy's arm."

"Good on you, Dick."

"Take care."

"Ta-ta."

Tucking in shirts and grasping swords and sticks, they ran off. Silas and Dick were left with the prisoners.

"You don't mind standing guard, do you?" Dick said. "Any trouble, give 'em a crack on the head. Don't think twice. They'd cut your throat soon as look at you." He touched Carver with a toe. "Specially this one."

With a malevolent eye Carver looked up at him.

Dick started up the gangway. "Right, Billy, into the fo'c'sle. Let's get this arm of yours cleaned up. See if we need to get you to a sawbones."

Silas looked down at the captives in his charge. They were a bloodthirsty quartet. He felt their gaze assessing him. Nervously he ran a tongue over his lips and smacked his cudgel into the palm of his hand.

Bosun, who had fled from the ferocity of the fighting, appeared along the jetty. Silas called and he came trotting to be patted and comforted.

There was a musical and familiar voice: "Silas! Silas!"

It was Ooli. Keeping an eye on his prisoners, Silas walked to the edge of the quay. Tail just moving, she floated beneath the bow of the *Morning Star*. "Are you all right?" he called.

"They shot at me but they missed." A rope ladder descended to the *Sea Urchin*. She grasped a rung and pulled herself on to the edge of the boat. "It has been so exciting! All your sailor friends and those men from the *Black Parrot*."

"They said you gave the alarm."

"Yes, I hear better than you." Her brow grew troubled. "But your lovely home! And your poor grandfather!"

"We'll be all right. At least we're both – "

He broke off to look at Bosun. Paws planted, he was barking ferociously at a stack of bales.

"Shut up, Bosun!"

But Bosun didn't shut up. Running forward, he nipped at the covering canvas and darted back. His barking redoubled.

"What is it, boy? A rat? Go on, you seek it out."

Silas looked at his prisoners. They too were watching Bosun.

"Just a minute," Silas said to Ooli and checked their ropes. None had produced another knife; the knots were secure. They looked up at him. One smiled. In Carver's eye there was a mocking expression.

"Noisy dog, that brute o' Jasper's," said a third ruffian. "What's he found there, a rat? Why'n't you go an' see? Shut 'im up."

Bosun ran forward again, clawing at the canvas.

"All right, boy." Tucking the club through his belt, Silas walked to the stack. "Good dog! Are you ready?"

The canvas had come loose. With both hands he seized a thick fold and tugged it back.

Silas was ready to stamp on a big rat or knock it from his clothes if it sprang at him. What he was not ready for was the red-bearded face of Jasper Dredge crouching between the bales and staring up with savage eyes. Albert was at his father's side, his fat cheeks white with fear.

For a split second nobody moved. Jasper's gaze flashed beyond Silas and saw that the quay was empty. Only the hated rag-and-bone boy stood there. With a snarl of rage he lunged with his rusty sword. Silas flung the canvas in his face and dashed away.

"Help!" he shouted at the top of his voice. "Help! Dick!"

Uttering oaths and threats, Jasper struggled from the heavy folds of canvas.

Silas fled. There was a blazing pain in his knee. He hardly felt it for close on his heels came Jasper, sword uplifted to split him from the crown of his head to his belly button.

Silas yelled again, dodging mooring ropes, and doubled back round pallets and a heap of anchor chain.

Albert ran to cut him off.

" 'Ere, Jasper!" roared one of the captives. "Never mind the boy. Cut us free."

"Else we're for the drop!"

"Yeah! Fix the 'snipe another time."

But Silas's shouts had found ears. The quay was not as empty as it appeared. Several ships distant, figures emerged where sailors from the *Morning Star* still hunted the waterfront for stragglers. Dick Chatham appeared on deck.

From the corner of his eye Jasper spotted them and halted in his pursuit. Right and left he looked along the quay, face livid with bites and choler. The sailors had seen him and came running swiftly. Survival was stronger than the wish for revenge.

"Albert! Quick, or they'll 'ave us!"

Abandoning his followers to their fate, he turned from the water and ran off through the piles of gear and cargo towards the warehouses.

They were halfway there when, from a narrow alley between the tall buildings, two more sailors appeared, pushing the surly figure of 'Ooky Sharp before them. The sailors were armed.

Jasper and Albert halted. 'Ooky, with his wrists bound and a rope hobbling his ankles, could be no help. They did not relish tackling the young sailors. Cornered, Jasper looked all round.

"Pa!" Albert shook with fright.

"Shut up, you little rat! Follow me."

They ran back to the water's edge. A few metres from the jetty the *Sea Urchin* drifted at the end of her line. The morning breeze had taken her from beneath the bow of the *Morning Star* into open water. The oars which the sailors had used lay along the side. If they could reach the dinghy they might row across the harbour. With the sailors closing in from all sides it was their only hope of escape.

Jasper nodded. "Right. Are you ready? One, two –"

"Pa!" Albert squealed. "I can't swim! You know I can't swim!" He grabbed his father's jacket.

"Cor! How'd I raise a useless article like you!" Jasper pulled his sleeve away and struck his son across the head. "Think on: it's the dinghy or the jail – an' likely the end of a rope for me. Which d'you want? Eh? You'll 'ave to swim!"

Albert was saved from answering, for at that moment the sleek head of Ooli broke the surface midway between the *Sea Urchin* and the spot where they stood. Her hair floated wide, the clear wavelets washed her shoulder. She looked up at the quay and in a moment realized the situation: a running sailor, the pair above her, the dinghy at her back.

She smiled.

Jasper Dredge gnashed his teeth. Savage emotions battled within him – fear and anger and revenge. The rat-bites made his face burn. With hot eyes he looked from the approaching sailors to the rowboat, his passport to safety. In five minutes he could cross the harbour and vanish in the maze of streets beyond. With a good start the sailors would never catch him. All that kept him from it was the little mermaid, that fishy piece of trouble on whose account he was now trapped.

"Arrggh! I'll soon fettle her!" Jasper threw aside his sword and pulled the dagger from his belt. "Albert, follow me. I'll see you don't drown. Now!"

With a roar he sprang from the quay, right on top of the floating mermaid.

The blow he struck at Ooli's slim figure would have sliced her to the heart. With a splash that hid everything for a moment, Jasper landed in the harbour. And when the spray cleared – the mermaid had gone.

Angry cries rose from the sailors who at that moment arrived above him.

Jasper twisted in the water and looked about him. The surface remained unbroken. With a wicked grin he shook his fist at the watchers on the quay.

"What she deserved!" he cried. "I filleted her! An' I'll do the same to any of you that gets in my way!"

Still clutching his dagger, he swam the few strokes that separated him from the waiting dinghy.

Suddenly, in a manner that took Jasper and everyone else by surprise, the water parted in front of him and

Ooli was back. Bright eyes stared into his own; white teeth parted in a laugh. With an oath, Jasper struck a second ferocious blow at her. Ooli darted aside. He lashed out again, carving the water with the razor-sharp blade. In an instant the quicksilver mermaid was behind him.

"Come, Jasper Dredge," she taunted. "Jasper the terrible. Hit me! Hit me!"

Jasper swam well for such a fat man. Spinning in the water, he struck again and again at the mermaid's head and silver tail. The dagger flashed past. In scatterings of bright spray, Ooli dodged from side to side. Springing into the air like a dolphin, she sailed over his head.

With shouts and laughter the sailors cheered her courage.

Then all at once – she was gone. Dagger raised and treading water, Jasper looked this way and that. He spun round – and spun back again. For a full minute he waited. The watching crowd fell silent. Where was the mermaid? Jasper looked from the quay to the drifting dinghy. Tentatively he began to swim in that direction.

Then suddenly – Jasper Dredge disappeared. One moment he was there; the next, almost before his face could register astonishment, he had gone. His raised dagger slipped silently beneath the water. Only a swirl on the surface marked the spot where he had been.

What happened underwater there was no way of

knowing. But half a minute later a slim arm emerged from the waves. No more, just an arm, holding Jasper's dagger aloft like the Lady of the Lake. The dagger was thrown to the quay. With a rattle it bounced across the cobbles.

The arm was withdrawn. The crowd waited. Some began to feel fear. It was one thing to cheer the mermaid, another to see a man drowned before their eyes, however wicked he might be.

Then the water parted beneath them, close to the quay, and Ooli emerged. Behind her she towed the fat figure of Jasper Dredge, spluttering and gasping for air. His arms and legs were bound with weed; from head to foot he was wrapped in a cocoon of fishing net from the bottom of the harbour.

"He's safe now," Ooli called to the sailors. "Throw down a line and pull him ashore."

She wove their rope through the net. The sailors heaved. Like a haul of haddock Jasper rose dripping from the water. Helplessly he scraped against the green stones of the harbour wall. As he recovered he began to struggle and swear again. The sailors dumped him roughly on the quay.

"You dogs!" Jasper raged and coughed water. "Untie me! By heaven, when I get free o' this I'll make you pay!"

Silas stood nearby, club in hand. Bosun was at his

side. Jasper regarded them with bulging eyes. Bound though he was, he flung himself at the boy's legs.

"This is your fault. All because o' you, a raggy street urchin. You wait till they find out in the Alleys. They'll cut your 'eart out! Eat your liver! Once they got me free again, I know punishments you've never dreamed of. I wouldn't be in your boots, not for a king's ransom." He struggled against the weed and fishing net. "Let me out o' this! Aarrgghh!"

While everyone watched the struggles of Jasper in the water, Albert Dredge had been largely forgotten. He had not been able to follow his father. Water, especially deep water like this, terrified him.

But Albert was cunning. As the sailors dragged his father from the tide and gathered round him on the quay, he took a slow step backwards. Nobody noticed. He took a second step and looked around.

There was no escape by running – everyone ran faster than Albert. He could not swim. The injured deck-boy sat at the head of the gangway of the *Morning Star* – but even if Albert succeeded in getting aboard, the sailors would follow and capture him. There seemed no way. Then his eyes fell upon the thick mooring ropes that led from bollards on the quay to the bow of the ship. One passed close by the pilot ladder that hung down to the *Sea Urchin*. If he could reach the dinghy, maybe he would succeed where his father had failed. It was either that or a long spell in jail. He looked from his trussed-up parent to the swords and sticks of the sailors – and took another step backwards.

It was Silas who spotted him creeping away. "Oh no you don't, Albert Dredge!" He ran forward.

Albert darted to the edge of the quay. It was half-tide and the mooring ropes hung slack. Quickly, to escape the sailors who began closing in, he seized the rope that ran past the pilot ladder and began to swarm along it.

At first he tried to crawl on top, fat knees on either side, the heavy rope against his chest and belly. He had not gone the length of himself, however, before he lost balance and swung beneath. To Albert's relief it turned out to be easier this way, hanging by his arms, legs crossed above the hemp. Steadily, hand over hand, he headed out from shore.

Silas limped to the end of the mooring line. He would have followed but his knee was too painful, and he could only watch as Albert drew further from the quay.

The sailors joined him.

Dick laughed. "He'll never make it."

He was right. For Albert was fat and out of condition, and the crawl was more tiring than he had anticipated. By the time he was halfway to the *Morning Star* he was panting with exhaustion. Moreover the rope steepened as it drew near the ship, and he had failed to take notice of a rat guard – a large disc clamped over the rope to prevent rats from running aboard from the harbour. No matter how he struggled, Albert could not get past. His arms ached, his shoulders felt pulled from their sockets. Too weary to crawl another metre, he hung above the water.

Then Silas took hold of the mooring rope and began to shake it – up and down, up and down – with all his skinny strength.

Albert cried aloud, showing his dirty teeth in terror as the thick rope lurched in his hands. Desperately he looked back at the quay.

"Stop it!"

A scatter of coins – Old Silas's savings – fell from his pocket. An empty pistol slipped from his belt. Splash! It followed the coins into the harbour.

"Will you come back?"

Albert did not reply.

Silas heaved and pushed again: up and down, up and down.

Albert wailed.

His fat body tossed beneath the leaping rope. Rolling his eyes, he looked beneath him. There waited the slim figure of the mermaid. Her tail curled in the deep water. Her eyes were wild.

"Thief!" Silas shouted angrily. "Pig! Destroyer! Look at our home!"

Orange flames still licked above the neighbouring roofs.

"Granda and me could have burned to death! I'll give you one last chance. Will you come back?"

"I can't!" Albert howled. He felt his fingers slipping. "Stop it! Stop it!"

"I hope she drowns you! Beast! Alley rat! It's what you deserve!"

Silas clenched his teeth and wrenched the rope back and forth.

Albert could hold on no longer.

"Aaaahhh! Aaaaaahhhhh!"

With a despairing cry he fell, twisting and sprawling, into the arms of the waiting mermaid.

There was a tremendous splash. And when the water cleared, both had gone.

Panting, Silas stared down at the bright waves beneath him.

Chapter Seventeen

The Red Sail

Albert was not drowned. A few minutes later, having given him a fright that he would never forget, Ooli towed him to a flight of stone steps. On hands and knees Albert crawled through weed to the handrail. Coughing water and blubbering with fear, he pulled himself to his feet.

Silas and the others looked down.

"Come on up," a sailor called.

Albert did not move.

The sailor descended and dragged him to the quay. Head hanging, he was dumped beside his father, 'Ooky Sharp and the other prisoners. His legs were bare for his trousers had split and come off in the underwater struggle. With tear-filled eyes he regarded Silas and the victorious sailors.

"Stop your snivelling!" snarled Jasper. "You're alive,

aren't you!"

"But Pa!" Albert rubbed his cheeks. "It's not fair, I can't swim. I could have been drowned. And it's freezing!" Water ran from his jacket. He pulled the tail of his shirt over fat knees. "What's going to happen now?"

"You're going to prison," said Dick Chatham. "You and your father. For a long time. That's what's going to happen now."

The sky was brightening. Beyond the rigging and tremendous breakwaters the first dot of sun sat golden on the horizon.

"Garh! No prison's 'eld me yet," said Jasper.

"This time's different," Dick said. "Most of your gang'll be in there with you."

Two of the sailors went through their clothes. Black as vultures and muttering angrily, the prisoners could not resist. Knives and knuckledusters, spikes, chains and razors rattled to the ground.

"You'll pay for this!" Jasper struggled. Flecks of spit clung to his whiskers. "All of you!"

Dick jammed a cork float on the hook at the end of 'Ooky's arm.

Silas saw Carver glance round the sailors and stretch his wrist. He pointed. "He's got something up his sleeve."

A sailor grabbed Carver's arm and pulled out a long thin dagger. Seven notches were cut in the handle.

Carver stared at Silas. If he had been free there is little doubt there would soon have been an eighth notch in the handle.

"On your feet!"

The surly prisoners did as they were told. Roped together like convicts, they were marched off to jail. They made a fine show of villains, cursing and struggling to the last.

At the end of the line, Jasper Dredge and Albert halted and stared back malevolently at the ragboy.

"We'll be back to see you, Silas Fisher!"

"Yeah, I wouldn't be in your shoes!"

"Chop y'up like dog-meat!"

The rat-bites were livid.

"Come on! That's enough lip from you two." A fresh-faced young sailor threatened them with a rope's end. "Tell your stories to the hangman."

"Aarrgghh!"

The line tightened and they were dragged forward by their companions. A minute later they reached the stacks of cargo, turned a corner and were gone from sight.

Up at the rag-and-bone yard, meanwhile, the fire still blazed. No fire engine, with ringing bell and galloping horses, attended that poor district. Neighbours passed buckets from hand to hand from the pump in the street. They managed to prevent the flames from spreading but the house and half the yard were gutted. By the time

Silas returned, the worst was past. A few small fires burned within, timbers glowed in the wind. In an hour their home had been reduced to a smoking shell. Nothing was saved. All their possessions, except the clothes they were wearing, a few piles of junk and a boat without mast or sail, had been destroyed.

"All right, Grandad." Dick laid a hand on the old man's shoulder. "Your friends will look after this. Come on down to the ship."

Silas and his grandfather were taken aboard the *Morning Star* and given a breakfast of bacon, fresh bread and coffee in the warm fo'c'sle.

"You've been up most of the night, the pair of you," said Dick. "You need sleep. Come on, Silas, you know where your hammock's stowed. Mr Fisher, you take this bunk here."

Old Silas was given a dry shirt. Soon, worn out by sickness and the events of the past few hours, he was sound asleep.

His grandson, rocking outside the circle of lamplight in the big cabin, pulled the blanket to his chin and watched and listened. Sailors were returning from the chase, some all the way from the Alleys. A few were wounded but none seriously. All had stories to tell. New arrivals shouted to shipmates. Laughter filled the fo'c'sle.

"Cor! I thought I'd 'ad me chips that time," called a blue-eyed able-seaman.

"I'm tellin' you," said another. "One o' them swords like the Turks 'ave. A big curved job. Take your 'ead right off!"

"You should've 'eard the language when we 'anded 'im over to the law," said a third. "Shockin'!"

Billy, the deck boy, sat with a jacket round his shoulders. His chest was bare, a blood-stained bandage covered his upper arm. "How many's that in prison now?" he said.

They made a count. "Nine," said somebody.

Dick looked towards Silas's hammock and saw that his eyes were closing. "Sshh!" He pointed. "Keep your voices down."

Exhausted by all that had happened – cast adrift, the hunt for Ooli, imprisonment in the *Black Parrot*, their escape, pursuit through the drains, the fire, the fight on the quay – Silas felt the fo'c'sle and talk of the sailors slip away. Pulling his face down into the blanket, he sank into a deep and healing sleep from which he did not emerge for nearly twenty-four hours.

He was awakened by soft voices and a bustle of preparation. Blinking, he saw sailors slip from their hammocks and pull on trousers and shirts. A few strapped swords round their waists. One primed a pair of pistols. He propped himself on an elbow and rubbed his face.

"Hey, Dick."

Several glanced towards him. Dick looked up from

buckling a shoe. "Oh, you've surfaced at last, have you."

The portholes were dark in the lamplight. "What's the time?"

"A bit after seven."

"Have I been asleep all day?"

"Not Sunday night." Dick laughed. "Seven on Monday morning."

"What!" Silas pushed down the bedclothes and swung his legs over the side of the hammock. "What's going on?"

"After what happened yesterday the Cap'n went to see the Chief of Police. There's been so much trouble in the Alleys an' with that *Black Parrot* gang, they're bringing in the Peelers from all around. First light this morning they're mounting a big raid, flush the crooks out once an' for all. Us boys are going along to see the fun. Cap'n give us the day off."

"Can I come?"

"Absolutely not!" Dick shook his head.

"Ah, please!" Silas jumped to the deck and winced as pain shot through his knee. "Come on, Dick!"

"No. It might be dangerous." He touched the stick thrust through his belt. "What d'you think we're carrying these for? If anything happened to you what would I tell your granda? 'Sides, it's halfway across the city an' you've got a bad leg. What if you had to run for it?"

Silas was crestfallen.

"'E could borrow Taffy the carter's old nag," said Billy, easing his injured arm into a jersey. "'E'll be alongside afore we leave."

"Who asked you to stick your oar in?" Dick said.

"Garn, don't be such an old misery," said Billy jauntily. "You can see 'e's set 'is 'eart on it." He pushed open a porthole and looked along the quay. "Yeah, there 'e is a'ready. Hey, Taffy, come 'ere a minute."

The walnut-faced old carter clip-clopped the length of the ship. "Hello there, Billy. Whoa!" The ramshackle cart drew to a halt.

Leaning from the porthole, Billy explained the situation. "So you'll lend Silas that ol' bag o' bones you call an 'orse, won't you?"

"Course, if 'e wants it. Do a favour for young Silas any time." The carter puffed on his broken clay pipe. "Don't want the poor old devil killed, mind."

Billy looked back into the cabin. "There, see. Nothin' to stop 'im."

"Can I come then?" said Silas. "Eh, Dick?"

The crew were on his side.

"Oh, I suppose so." Dick gave way. "But on condition. You stay close by me all the time. An' take that club with you, just in case." He scrubbed Silas's hair with a rough hand. "Go on, then. We haven't got all day."

The carter's horse was white, its head hung low and its ribs stuck out. But as Silas rode bareback through the city streets among the sailors, something of the occasion communicated itself to the old animal. Its head came up, its ears pricked and it glared around with rheumy eyes. Every so often, for reasons of its own, it whinnied wildly, showing long yellow teeth, alarming everybody nearby.

Silas's hair blew in the November wind. In one hand he held the greasy reins, in the other a thick dripping sandwich. His knee throbbed painfully but his thick blue jacket and trousers were warm. As he rode at Dick's side he felt like a king.

The sky was clear and the sun was just rising as they reached the square in the city centre. Massed police and several score of soldiers were assembled there, all in uniform and armed.

"Right, men." The senior officer addressed them. "You've had your orders, you know what to do. Clear the scum out of the Alleys, make the city a safe and decent place for honest men and their families. There'll be dirty fighting, so keep an eye in the back of your heads. Look out for your comrades."

In fighting units of twenty and thirty, followed by the sailors with Silas in their midst, they marched on the wicked Alleys.

The battles of that day in Wolf Lane, Rum Alley, Throttle Close and Jamaica Row; the fighting in the narrow streets; the struggles on the twisting stairs and across the wilderness of rooftops; the clashes of sword and bayonet, the volleys of muskets, have passed into legend. So too have the exploits of Ooli, the little mermaid, who swam upstream and kept watch on the broad river. For several outlaws tried to escape by water but not one made it to the opposite bank.

By midday the police and soldiers had fought their way to the heart of the Alleys, to the notorious *Black Parrot* tavern in Hangman Square. Silas watched, astride his horse, as with fiery torches it was set ablaze. The rotting timbers flared. Casks of rum exploded. Bales of smuggled silk, flaming high, bowled across the pavement. Hidden hoards of gold and jewels pattered into the inferno.

By mid-afternoon the battle was over. Captives, bound hand and foot, were flung on to carts and driven away to prison. There were so many that the city jails could not hold them all, so the most dangerous – Jasper and Albert among them – were marched off to an ancient fortress and locked away in the dungeons.

But three gallows-birds were never captured. Blind Nancy, in her moth-eaten fur coat, accompanied by Eli Clutch and Pinky, managed to evade their pursuers. Late that night – with jewelled rings, ropes, knives and a bagful of meat pies – they ambushed a coach at the edge of the city. Lashing the horses into foam, coach-wheels leaping in the potholes, they set off for another part of the country.

It was as if a great fresh wind had swept through the Alleys. Armies of cleaners moved in with brooms, sacks of flea-powder and terriers to kill the rats. They burned sulphur in disease-ridden chambers and poked out the cobwebs and fungus. Rubbish was carted away. The streets were hosed clean.

That night Silas joined Dick and the crew of the *Morning Star* in the *Jolly Jack Tar* and drank more ale than was wise for a boy of his age. The sailors tied ribbons in their caps and sang loud sea songs. He had a wonderful time. At midnight, light-headed and hiccuping, he accompanied them back to the fo'c'sle.

"Oh, Granda! I wish you'd been there." Clutching a mug of hot ship's cocoa, he sat by the stove as they told his grandfather their adventures.

Ooli climbed the pilot ladder which hung from the bow. Happily she sat on a wooden rung and watched through an open porthole. A chill wind blew from the sea. At her back the ships and harbour were bathed in moonlight.

"Go on, Dick," urged Silas. "Tell him – hic! – about the bayonet charge. And that room full of loot under the church."

Above the rim of his mug he watched Bosun and Sweep. In the cruel world of the *Black Parrot* the dog had never learned to play. Now, in the safety of the fo'c'sle, the little cat teased him into a game of chase. Here and there, over bunk and chair and sea-chest, Sweep bounded like a black streak. Wuffing and excited, the clumsy dog romped in pursuit.

"Hey! Watch out!" Dick slopped ale down his trousers.

Instantly Bosun stopped his play and cowered to the deck, waiting for the blow that never came.

"All right, old chap." Dick patted the wrinkled head. "No one's going to hurt you."

"Sorry. Hic! Come here, Bosun."

Believing he had done wrong, the dog slunk to Silas's side.

"That's a good boy. Lie down by me now."

Obediently Bosun curled up on a scrap of canvas and laid his head upon his paws. One eyebrow raised, he watched the cheeky Sweep who shuffled his paws and pounced upon his yellow tail. Rolling over, the little cat battled with it as though it were a rat. When even this did not tempt his new-found playmate to resume the game, Sweep touched Bosun with his nose and curled up against his side.

"What do you think will happen to them, Granda?" Silas said a while later. "Jasper Dredge and Albert, and all the – hic! – rest of them?"

There was no answer. His grandfather had fallen asleep in his chair. He was ill. The fire and exertion had been too great.

"Leave him be." Dick tucked a blanket round the old man's waist. "Time you were in your hammock anyway, young Silas. Your eyes are closing. Come on."

Silas rose.

"Good night," called Ooli.

"Ni-ight!" He flapped a hand. The cocoa had not overcome the effects of the ale. Staggering slightly, he left the circle of lamplight for the shadows of his hammock. He wished his head did not feel so peculiar. Fumbling with the buttons, he pulled off his jacket and dropped it on the deck, kicked off his trousers. It had been a momentous day. With grubby fingers he smoothed the portrait of his father and set it on an orange-box beside the carved knife which he had recovered from Albert that morning. Awkwardly he clambered into bed.

"Goo'night, Dick. Night – hic! – everybody."

"Good night, lad. Happy dreams."

And no sooner had his head hit the pillow than Silas was sound asleep.

By noon the next day he had recovered from his hangover – and his knee soon healed for Silas was young. But his grandfather was weak. That night, and for days afterwards, Old Silas tossed and turned in a fever. A doctor was summoned. Ooli, who had the healing powers of her people, swam far out to sea for weeds and shellfish to make medicines, but in those cold waters she could not find the ingredients she needed.

Silas was anxious; the doctor's report had not been good. What if his grandfather were to die – his granda whom he loved so much. Would he be given a pauper's meagre funeral? And what would happen to *him*? He had no other relatives. Would he be left to sleep in doorways and under carts in the market? Might he be taken to the dreaded poorhouse? Or when, as he prayed, his grandfather recovered – where would they live? They had nothing. Time and again as he worked with the sailors about the ship, he ran back to the fo'c'sle to keep his grandfather company and see if he needed anything.

Late one morning he sat with Ooli on the foredeck, close to the fo'c'sle door. Slings of cargo swung aboard from the busy quay. Sailors with paintbrushes and coils of new rope swarmed about the ship.

"The *Morning Star* will sail soon," said Ooli. "Your sailor friends will be gone, far away to the land of snow and floating mountains. It is time for me to leave also." She drew a pretty brush through her hair and examined her face in a mirror. They were presents from the sailors. "What will you do? Your house has gone, you have no money. The winter will get worse – sleet and frost and snow."

For a week Silas had thought of little else. "I don't know." His brow was furrowed.

"Well, you must decide." Ooli's eyes were clear as the ocean. "There *is* a way out of your troubles. It would make me happy – and this way, I know, your grandfather would grow strong again."

Old Silas had woken. After the days of sleep and warmth he felt a little better. At the sound of their voices he rose from his bunk and pulled a blanket round his shoulders. Shakily he walked to the door of the fo'c'sle. Silas and Ooli did not see him at their backs.

"You must come with me to the Islands of the Sun," said the little mermaid. "My father will make you welcome. But the journey is long and dangerous. I shall be there to protect you, but where I swim there will sometimes be storms. Sharks will surround your boat. Giant octopuses will reach out of the waves. It is no voyage for the faint-hearted. Have you the courage?"

Silas drew his thin wrists into the warmth of his jersey and shivered.

"Do you need to ask him that?"

They turned in surprise.

Old Silas gripped the frame of the door. His blanket blew in the breeze. "Are you still a prisoner in that mouldy cellar? Did we die in the fire? He might have the body of a skinny rag-and-bone boy but he has the heart of a lion." He struggled for breath. "Well, Silas? Do you want to eat mangoes and dive into lagoons and watch the sun through palm trees? Or shall we stay here and find some corner to huddle away from the cold?"

Silas looked from his grandfather to the mermaid, and back again.

"I know what I think." Old Silas coughed and pushed the hair from his eyes. "But we're asking you."

Silas hesitated then gave a barely perceptible nod. "Yes," he whispered.

"Yes, what?" said his grandfather.

"We'll go." He thought. "But it's a long way. Is the *Sea Urchin* big enough?"

"She is a strong boat," Ooli said. "A good boat. She rides the sea well. I saw how you sailed out to the island when we went fishing. With my help you will arrive safely."

"Good." Old Silas smiled faintly. "That's settled then." He retreated into the fo'c'sle. "I think I could drink some beef tea now. Don't worry about me, boy. I'm tough as an old nut." Cough! Cough! "I'll survive."

"Oh, Silas!" Ooli was excited. "It will be wonderful. It will be an *adventure*!"

On hands and tail she lolloped across the deck. "Dick!" she shouted loudly. "Dick! Come here! Everybody – listen! Silas and his granda are coming home with me. We're all going to the Islands of the Sun!"

★ ★ ★

For a week there was a bustle of preparation. Silas checked the *Sea Urchin* and gave her a fresh coat of paint and tar. The sailors stitched a set of red sails and rigged her with a new mast and oars. Flotation canisters were lashed to the sides. The doctor prescribed ten bottles of medicine for Old Silas. A little stove was found, and sets of oilskins and sou'westers. Fresh water containers were stowed beneath the seats. Biscuits and fruit and dried meat were wrapped securely.

Silas and Dick spent hours together. Dick was like a big brother to him and a son to Old Silas.

The weather turned cold. The wind blew from the north and brought flurries of snow. Ice covered the deck of the *Morning Star*. In the warm fo'c'sle, Old Silas knitted his grandson a balaclava and a pair of fingerless gloves.

And early one morning, with the little mermaid leaping alongside, the *Sea Urchin* set sail from the brown city. The quay was lined with friends; the rails and rigging of the great ships were crowded with sailors.

"Safe voyage!" they cried. "Come back and tell us your adventures!"

"We will." Silas hoisted the new sail. "When I'm older and Granda is strong. We'll rebuild the house and yard. We'll buy a horse. We'll have a party!"

The sailors cheered. Chocolate and apples rained down into the boat.

"Goodbye, my friends." Muffled in warm rugs and a tarpaulin, Old Silas waved. "Thank you for everything."

"Good luck!"

"Goodbye!" Silas's shrill voice rang across the water.

Bosun and Sweep looked over the bow. The dog cocked his head to one side.

"Ooli, look!" Silas pointed.

A single rat, sleek in the water, paddled busily towards the shore. The mermaid laughed and let it go.

The sail filled. Leaning to one side, the little boat picked up speed. Seabirds circled overhead. A wintry sun pulled clear of the clouds and cast a track across the sea, right between the curving breakwaters. Further and further the *Sea Urchin* headed out from land, silhouetted against that great light.

A faint cry drifted back against the wind, and suddenly the watchers on shore saw that the surface of the sea about the boat was dotted with seals. Porpoises sprang to port and starboard. Leaping higher than any, her long hair flying, the little mermaid led the procession.

Silas looked back as they passed beneath the lighthouse, then forward into the dazzling sun. With a smile to match it, Ooli looked up from the water. Eagerly she pointed, arm outstretched.

"South, Silas!" she cried. "Turn south!"

Silas grasped the tiller with a thin hand.

The bows slid round. The north wind filled the sails. Ahead lay the open sea, and whales and flying fish and coconuts, and the Islands of the Sun.